Down is Up

Down is Up

Ruth Dalglish

Down is Up
Published by Ruth Dalglish
loire@kinect.co.nz

© 2019 Ruth Dalglish

ISBN 978-0-473-48631-0 (Softcover)
ISBN 978-0-473-48632-7 (ePUB)
ISBN 978-0-473-48633-4 (Kindle)

Typesetting:
Andrew Killick
Castle Publishing Services
www.castlepublishing.co.nz

Cover design:
Paul Smith

Contents

Chapter One

The big house lay back elegantly across its broad garden. Light flowed from every window, defining graceful trees wearing the pale blossom of early summer. Smart cars were parked on the wide drive which descended gently to the road. More cars were parked in the shade of dark trees, where a faint perfume of orange blossom invited one to linger, even in the cooling night air. Pleasant music drifted into the quiet night.

A couple were walking hand in hand up the hill. He commented, "Looks like Howard's having a party. Celebrating his success I guess. Wow! Look at those cars! Citroen, Jaguar, Mercedes, BMW."

She said, "Lucky blighters. How do they get so rich?"

"We're all Kiwis aren't we? We all work. Nobody should be rich."

"I think he's not too mean; supports some of the sports teams. She's keen on music, thinks herself a patron of the arts."

"So that's what we can hear."

"Yeah, something classical."

They had walked a hundred meters up the road, when a shocking noise split the calm night. An ambulance siren stopped at the big beautiful house. Excited voices were raised, to bring faces to the windows of neighbouring houses. "It's here! What's happening!"

The ambulance parked near the front door. While the guests gaped, wide-eyed, the medics spoke to Howard, efficiently examined Mr Cobbold and carried him out to the ambulance. Howard tried to comfort the weeping Mrs Cobbold as he drove her to the hospital. The guests, embarrassed, spoke little and took leave of Marilyn at the door. The musicians soberly packed their instruments. Expensive motors, almost silent, slid away down the hill. Only the fairy lights adorning the trees continued to glow, reminders of the party that was.

Marilyn, feeling numb, turned their switch off, dowsed some of the house lights and closed the piano lid. Gordon, her son, and his wife Tracy lingered to help her tidy away the wine glasses and food litter on the tables.

"We have to get home to relieve our baby sitter," said Gordon. "But we'll talk tomorrow and help you all we can. Let us know what's happening."

"Thank you so much," said Marilyn as she kissed Tracy and exchanged hugs.

Howard arrived home a little later, silent, except to say in answer to her query, "He's dead. I rang their family. They'll help Mrs Cobbold."

There seemed nothing more to say. They retired and woke late the next morning, Saturday. Both had feelings of dissatisfaction and shock. The celebration had turned sour, and they felt that somehow Cobbles had brought bad luck by planning the party. Howard went into the office to check on the jobs which were to be completed on Friday. Mari felt limp. The memories of last night replayed in her mind like a horror movie, at odds with the bright morning sun. The crash of a falling body, people gasping in shock, as conversation died; Howard trying to take control and phoning the ambulance, which arrived like a late guest but an unwelcome one. Mari wished that the bad dream would end; that she could sink through the floor. But the end would be disaster.

Distractedly, Mari began to tidy the kitchen until a knock at the door announced the arrival of Mrs Mac, the cleaning lady. Her eyes were gleaming with obvious curiosity. Mari tried to answer her questions, knowing that her words would be repeated all over the district by evening. Also, knowing that a recital was scheduled for that afternoon, she began to plan what to say in answer to the inevitable questions. I'll try to smile sweetly and play it down, saying how sad for Mrs Cobbold.

With difficulty they got through the weekend. Howard played golf, rather indifferently, with his friends. Mari tried to lighten the time by inviting Tracy, Gordon and the children to visit on Sunday. She cooked some special items for them, and was rewarded by their appreciation. The children worked their usual magic although Monday was hanging over their grandparents. Howard rose early on Monday, saying that he needed to be there before the staff.

Howard arrived home while Mari was cooking dinner. He looks awful she thought, reaching up to kiss him. "Had a bad day?" she asked.

"Stinking," he said. His face looked ten years older. "Everyone knew, when I arrived. 'What's going to happen?' they ask. The girls are in a tizzy. The managers are very solemn, looking at me as though I'm the almighty. I wish I were. The accountant is plainly worried. It seems that something is very wrong. Cobbles' P.A. is missing. The accountant says we have to be very careful and get the auditors in tomorrow."

Mari felt her facial muscles contract while she blanched. "What's happened?" she whispered, fearing the answer. "Was it … embezzling?" The word was like a death-threat.

"Probably."

"Why?"

"I can only guess Cobbles was too fond of gambling, or some such thing. Some time ago someone mentioned a race horse. He might have half owned one."

"Gosh, that's shocking." In Mari's family gamblers were thought to be foolish, at the very least. To own a race horse one had to be incredibly rich. "I'm horrified that a man you trusted would do such a thing. Is the loss serious? What will happen to us?"

"You and me personally? We cut down. The firm? I don't know until investigations are done. Then, can we pay the wages? I'll be the first to be hit. Tough luck for us. If the bank balance isn't all it should be, we'll have to cut back; economise; at the same time not letting it be admitted to other people. Avoid contracts which will be too gross on the outlay."

"I'm scared for you." She pulled a chair closer and put her arm around him.

"I'm scared too."

"I know! I'll sell my jewellery. You must have spent a lot on me."

Howard smiled grimly. "Thank you honey. But hold onto it in the meantime. We might need it to pay the butcher. We have to keep a phone. Contacts are vitally important." He paused. "I'll have to tell the guys I won't be playing golf for a little while. Green fees are too expensive. I won't tell them that but they'll probably guess." He sat, mouth drawn down while he slumped in his chair. The phone rang. Howard answered, "Hullo Gren." He spoke in monosyllables as he listened to the accountant.

Mari rose and stirred the meal that gave out appetising smells. Tears came to her eyes as she saw her husband's distressed face. He doesn't deserve this. I know it can't be his fault. I wonder what Cobbles' wife is thinking now. She'll be in a worse state than I am.

He spent most of the evening on the phone to this and that adviser, pausing briefly to eat the dinner she placed before him, and drinking a glass of wine in silence. This used to be a pleasant part of their day. Mari's phone was untypically silent. Her friends probably didn't know what to say. Usually they planned their activities in the evening.

Now I'm no one, she thought. Misfortune can be catching. I'm alone here.

The next morning Howard was frowning as he poured milk on his cereal. "One of the first things to do is to sell the house."

Marilyn gasped. "Sell this house? You surely don't mean it? Where would we live?" Her heart was beating hard, her face flushed. "We bought that beach cottage you liked. We'll have to live there." "But we can't live in it, not yet! It's got one bedroom and one small bathroom. You know we plan to extend it; make a much bigger kitchen and living room, two more beds, shower and toilet..."

"I'm sorry, it's there or nowhere. Count yourself lucky to have a roof to keep the rain out. It's better than a tent. Extensions will be in the future if at all."

Marilyn fell silent. By looking at his face and his drooping shoulders she realised this was no time to complain. Howard walked to the garage. She heard the car start and drive off. In an unhappy daze she automatically cleared the dishes. A glance at the clock made her remember that she had to ring Mrs Mac and tell her that she could no longer employ her. My name will be mud. I'll have to give her a bonus. In five minutes my words will be all over the town. Sourly, the thought came that it will easier to do the housework in so tiny a house, but hopefully with a few improvements.

Chapter Two

The future tasks of packing up and moving took her breath away. Listlessly she cleaned the kitchen, then walked through the rest of the house. It had ten rooms, of well-chosen furniture (what fun it had been buying it), cupboards full of chattels, wardrobes of clothes; an impossible task. She sat at the piano and played it for five minutes, then, despairing, closed the lid. It was a relief when the phone rang. Gordon's wife, Tracy, spoke, "Marilyn," in such a sympathetic voice that Mari almost cried. "Tracy dear, I'm so glad it's you. Have you heard?"

"Yes. Gordon told me. We are both very shocked."

"Dear, I feel lost. I don't know what I'm doing. Howard says we have to sell the house. I just can't think…"

"Mari, love, I can understand. I'm so sorry you've had this terrible ultimatum, well, flung at you. Would you like me to drop in after I leave Danny at kindergarten?"

"Oh yes, yes. Please do. I'd love to talk to you."

The day was still sunny, the flowers and trees just as beautiful as Marilyn looked out, but she felt cruel thoughts dragging at her mind, as though to a prison. It's the end of this.

Upstairs she found some jeans and old clothes after a quick shower. Through the bedroom windows she saw Tracy's car. Running downstairs she met her and baby Melissa at the door. They hugged, silent, until Mari turned her gaze to her grand-daughter.

"What a honey you are, darling. Got a kiss for Grandma?" The cherubic smile warmed her heart as Melissa came to her arms.

"Tracy, it's so good of you to come. Shall we sit for a minute if you have time to talk?"

"Of course. You know we're really distressed about your predicament. I just came to offer help if I can."

"It's such a relief to talk to you. This is an impossible situation." With a rueful laugh she said, "If you've any helpful thoughts please share them with me. I feel I'm running round like a wet hen. I'm Mrs A. in her beautiful house, and Howard says we have to sell it. Raise money immediately!"

The practical Tracy said, "Where will you live?"

"Howard says it's lucky we have the beach house, tiny as it is."

They discussed the cottage and what furniture could possibly be fitted into it, then wandered upstairs to the main bedroom, seen in some disorder. The open door of the big wardrobe revealed the shimmer of silky evening gowns, lines of smart day clothes and shoe racks in all colours.

Mari said, "I'm ashamed that I've bought so many expensive clothes. Madame de Lyons used to ring me so gushingly. 'Mrs Alton, we've just received a new range of imported frocks. Some of them look just right for you. Would you like to come in to have first choice?'"

Bitterly, Mari said, "And I fell for it, all that flattering talk. What a fool I was."

"It's easy to see why she said it. You've got the figure that shows off any dress. She used you to advertise her shop."

"I've got the horrible feeling she's not the only one. Howard used to look at me every time I wore a new frock when we went to posh dos and met his business friends and non-friends. He used to say, 'I like that one on you. It's plain to see that I'm a success and I'll make more success for someone. You're good for me, my darling.' How stupid I was!"

"That's not your fault. It's probably true, when all the facts are counted."

"Mmm," said Mari, flopping to sit on the dressing table stool. "What do I do with these gorgeous expensive evening things? I can't keep them in the cottage."

"Let me think about it. I've a friend who has a nearly-new shop in another big town. She might be able to sell some for you. I could keep one or two frocks for you. It might be possible to store some furniture until – well, you will have a future, I'm sure. Just keep practical stuff."

Little Melissa had followed, clutching her doll and her Mum's hand. They sat on the unmade bed until Mari noticed the time and said, "I'll make the bed and tidy here then we'll go down for coffee and a biscuit." Together they straightened the sheets. Mari said, "Perhaps someone would like to buy the furniture with the rooms. This Queen Anne suite is far too grand for the cottage."

"I agree with you. You and Howard have suited the furniture to the house perfectly."

Back in the kitchen, Mari started the cafetiere. Melissa was sitting at the table drinking a cup of milk, careful not to spill any. "She's coming on well with this," said her proud Mum. "Are you expecting Howard? I think his car's arriving."

Howard tramped heavily into the kitchen, kissing Mari and Tracy quickly. "And who's this come to visit?" He picked up his grand-daughter and swung her high, smiling into her big blue eyes. She crowed with pleasure and he cuddled her on his knees. They all relaxed in the pleasure of the moment. Mari thought it was possible to ask him, gently, about progress.

"Yes, I've talked to land agents. They're sure we'll get a good injection of cash, which is what we need. They'll advertise it in the main centres, possibly try to auction after that. We have to move out soon anyway. We have to pay the mortgage and sell the big car."

He tried to smile at his wife, the sun accentuating the worry lines round his eyes. "You're a good mate. What say we buy a couple of bikes?"

"And we can share the car on wet days." She tried to smile in return. Tracy admired their control. "I'll help all I can," she told her mother-in-law.

"After we move out I'll get a job; take pupils which is what I'm qualified for, if we can organise a place for a piano. Wouldn't be room in the cottage."

"I have meetings this afternoon with a lawyer and a bank manager. Tomorrow's the funeral for old Cobbles."

"I'm glad you told me," said Mari. "I'll have to order flowers to be delivered,"

"Pity. I'd rather not spend money on him."

"We're obliged, and it may help to comfort Mrs C. Do you think she knows the enormity of what he has done?"

"I haven't told her. She'll guess sooner or later by the talk."

"Poor woman," said Mari, but to herself she thought, she may have to sell her house now. They sat silently for a few minutes, broken only by the murmuring of the little girl, trying to feed a biscuit to her doll, while safely held on Grandad's knee. He kissed her.

"Precious girl. You won't suffer for someone's mistakes."

"She's not suffering now," said Tracy firmly. "You two have been wonderful grandparents and I'm sure you'll continue to be." Rising, she said, "I think I had better get going 'cause I have shopping to do before I pick up Danny. I'll try to find a suitable home for your piano."

"Give him a kiss from us and our love," said Mari. They all walked to the car. Tracy buckled Melissa into her seat, saying, "I'd love to help you, Mari. Just ring. I'll come any morning while Danny's at kindy."

"You're a sweetie, thank you dear. I do appreciate it." They waved, laughing at Melissa who was trying to send them kisses. For that moment the sadness was lifted.

Early evening found Marilyn very tired. She'd obtained boxes and filled them with books and special treasures, accumulated over the years. Whatever do I do with the stuff left behind by the children? Gordon had his own home and space, perhaps, but Rodney and Sylvia were renting, with limited room for extras. The phone rang and she answered wearily. Rodney's voice exploded in her ear. He sounded angry. "I must talk to Dad. Is he there ?"

"I'll call him." Howard took the phone. It seemed that their son was almost shouting, while Howard responded quietly without emphasis. He hung up and turned to the kitchen, where Mari was preparing dinner.

"He's blaming me that, quote, 'I've allowed this to happen'. It's easy for him to talk. Surely I'd have stopped Cob if I'd suspected but he's been a clever chap and used two or three people in and outside the firm to conceal his doings; probably bribed them as well. If he hadn't died suddenly we would not have known, at least for a time. Possibly got away with it." Howard's normally mild voice was cracking. Mari tried to soothe him with the offer of food.

"You'll feel better if you eat," she said.

"I don't want it." He stomped off to his office. The spicy smell of beef curry remained in the kitchen.

Marilyn couldn't stop her tears of fatigue and grief. "I've got no one, father or mother, to comfort me or tell me how to help my husband. I'm alone."

After Howard's departure next morning, Marilyn tried to think how to manage her work. Her phone used to be always busy, with people needing her to take important parts in this or that activity, but not now. She made vain attempts to reach her precious daughter Sylvia, who was on holiday somewhere with her architect husband. Thank goodness we got the wedding over before this happened. The children are grown and self-supporting, That's a blessing, thank God.

The ghastly day of the funeral was over. The managers in the firm took brief time to attend it while work went on as usual. Tradesmen have responsibilities and deadlines to meet. A formal service in a church was followed by a reception in which the attendees were dourly received. Hidden rumours had nurtured an atmosphere of unease, with many shifty glances. Conversations were stilted and kind words few. At the end was only relief. Marilyn and Howard had arrived home to shed their funeral clothes and pick up the urgent tasks.

Now Marilyn was feeling more depressed than ever, angry with herself for her lack of a thought-out plan. Howard had heaps of work, and his managers to confer with. Mari's mother lived in the U.S. of A. with her new husband. I wonder what time I can ring her, she asked herself. Perhaps this evening? I know. I'll have a good look at the beach cottage and work out what to do first. So I'll drive down and try to persuade Tracy to come. She'll surely have good suggestions, with all her Home Science training.

A little later they were on their way to the coast. The chatter of the children lifted, as usual, Marilyn's heart. "I'm so glad you could spare me the time for this," she said as they drove the narrow road to the cottage. "I know it's not the most beautiful beach when the tide's out and the stones are showing, but there's something I like about the setting and the view."

"I agree with you. It has charm. A very small beach but that means fewer people and more privacy for you. Your house is sheltered from the south wind by the little hill at the back and the big trees behind it. A good choice, I'd say. I've brought a tape measure and a pen so you can work out what will fit in where."

Danny shouted "Yippee," and ran towards the beach as they piled out. Mari unlocked the porch door. They were met by the somehow pleasant smell of a wooden beach house.

"I can see why you bought it," said Tracy. They discussed the possibilities and admired the sea view from the north-facing windows. "When you bring the utilities from your own kitchen it could easily become practical."

"Yes, with more power points in place. I'm sure Howard will do that, in fact he'll probably check the wiring and replace it. So long as the roof is sound. But men know what to look for. I hope he has free time in the next weekend. He can send a man to do the wiring."

They noted measurements until Tracy said, "Whoops! Where's Melissa?" She rushed outside to look, and returned from the back of the section with her daughter. "Did you know you have fruit trees? An orange which has flowered recently and has tiny baby oranges, and a plum tree with little green fruit."

"Oh wonderful!" said Mari. "Something to look forward to, and free."

"Yes, fruit trees are so giving. Now, have we done enough measuring?"

"Yes, I think so. I have a bit more hope and a list of needful things. I know we must go home to cook dinner." They locked up and called Danny, who said, wiping sand off his hands, "This is a beaut place. Can I come again Grandma?"

"Yes, of course, come lots of days and bring your shovel and trucks. I'll make your lunch."

Marilyn arrived home with some euphoria, which she relayed to her husband over dinner. He brightened a little. "That's a good girl. I knew I could rely on you."

"How are things going at work?"

"Not too badly. For the moment we can pay the wages. The sale of our big car should help if I get a good price."

"And can we use a little, just a little bit, to bring the cottage to a better standard?"

"I hope so. I can send a man to do the wiring. We need to be safe." With that Mari knew she had to be content for the time being.

The next morning Marilyn woke with purpose in her mind. She did the minimum of housework to keep the house looking beautiful for possible buyers; though the land agents were looking country-wide to attract larger money, for their own selfish motives. There were likely to be warning phone calls of such a visit. The day for the auction was still not set. Problems about disposal of many items were not yet resolved.

"My piano," she mourned. "How can I use it to teach?"

Wearing jeans and a back pack, she took her bicycle to the biggest hard-ware store, with a list of small necessities for the beach house. It was a foreign place to her, and she had to ask an assistant often for guidance. At last, with a full bag, she stood waiting near the checkout counter. An elderly woman in front of her turned from the counter and brushed her slightly.

The lady apologised, then said, looking into Mari's eyes, "I know you. You're Marilyn. I knew you when you were a young girl. My favourite pupil. May I meet you outside when you've finished in here?"

Mari nodded, a little puzzled, searching her brain. Still thinking, she found her long-ago friend waiting.

"Marilyn dear, I'm Winifred Meldrum, a Sunday school teacher that was." The soft, gentle voice and smile were familiar, the hair gray but still curly. She had a motherly, slightly plump figure. "I longed to know how you were finding life. You had such bright, intelligent eyes; a lovable child." To Marilyn the motherliness was like ointment on burned skin.

"Of course! Mrs Meldrum, you were so kind to us all. Pity we had to grow up and leave you."

"That's how I feel too. Can I ask you, dear, how you're getting on? Now I've found you I don't want to lose you."

"The story's so long. I'd love to talk to you but; well…"

"How about coming back to my house, for a bite of lunch today. I'd love you to come. My car's here."

"I don't know where you live. I came here on a bike…"

"I'm sure we can fix that problem. Please come."

An hour later they were sitting on the deck of Win's house, facing her flower garden, and eating the promised basic lunch with home-made lemonade. It was a pleasant feast for two friends.

"Thank you for coming, Marilyn. I'm so glad to have you here. Do call me Winifred or Win."

"Thank you Win. I'm so thankful to be here. I'm relaxing for the first time in days."

"I do gather that there's cause for worry in your life. If it would help you to talk, please do."

"Oh, Win, I shouldn't burden you. But I do feel ghastly and alone in all these difficulties. I don't know where to begin. The worst is that Howard is terribly worried about the financial state of the firm. You may have heard that his partner died, suddenly. He was a gambler, embezzling the firm's money. The auditors have confirmed that some rainy-day deposits of money have disappeared."

"At least Howard has you being supportive and that's a plus. Tell me the whole story, unless you want to keep it secret."

"It would be a relief to tell you. I know I can trust you." To her shame she felt tears trickling down her face. She sniffed into a hanky, while Win found her a box of tissues.

"My darling girl. You surely need help."

Mari thought for a moment. "Well, it has always been a wonderful marriage. You might have known I was into music and dancing, successfully. Howard saw me dancing, fell in love and insisted on marrying me. I was only eighteen. And so I was a mother of two when I was twenty one. No time then for music or dancing. But Howard was very good to me and got someone to help me when they were babies. He was ambitious and thought it best to go into partnership with Cobbles, I mean Mr Cobbold, a somewhat older man. The business was thriving. Howard had a flair for it, and he was good at attracting clever tradesmen."

"So your husband was more than an electrician ?"

"Yes, he certainly had imagination and could think past the daily jobs. Whatever people needed for working conditions, comfort, safety, luxury; specialised departments could be built into the firm, and clever advertising might persuade many to include in the building a lot of costly improvements. That would need more capital to begin with, and that's where Cobbles came in, as a partner." The stress was showing on Mari's face, and Win encouraged her to rest for a minute. She ate a few biscuits and drank another glass of lemon.

"Yes. The firm was growing, and that's about the time I was brought into the picture. Howard wanted a wife to complete his happiness. He was fairly outgoing, enjoying the company of people and had a number of friends. Some were those you would call middle class but leading to the more affluent. We were invited to visit, and I accompanied him as often as possible, that is, when pregnancy did not prevent me. We began to entertain his friends occasionally, then more often. We were sucked into this 'money culture.' As I said, Howard was good at making friends, and I, at his side, was quite ornamental. He and Cobbles said it was good for the business." After a reflective pause, she said, "I think Mrs C was not comfortable when trying to entertain people, and so they relied on me mainly to be hostess. That was not too difficult, as Howard allowed me to employ help when necessary, including a nanny for the children. I had a third child, a little girl, so after I slimmed again I could wear the right clothes and be the pretty wife." She sighed. "It was becoming like a performance, a somewhat shallow one. Cultivate the right people, say the flattering words, when underneath the words the feelings could be rather mean and critical. I learned more about some of these people than I wanted to know. I tried to be sincere and kind when the children were present. But it's hard not to let that atmosphere permeate your life, and somehow the children will be affected. I knew it was wrong. We had the wrong standards. I was trying to live a double life, being a good person like my parents were but now mixing with yuppies and making money. Music was always a fine goal but I'm noticing now that I do what seems right for the wrong reasons."

"I did meet your mother once or twice, and I thought she was a good woman. Where is she now?"

"Well, after Daddy died she lived alone for some years, then met another kind, decent man. They married, lived here for a while but he wanted to go to the U.S. of A. because that's where his children were living. For his sake she went there too, and she knew I was safely married to Howard." Mari's voice broke in a sob. "I so long for someone I could lean on, who would tell me what to do."

"Tell me, what do you feel you should be doing?"

"Helping Howard, I suppose, by earning money. He says he can't draw a salary from the firm because there's not enough and the workers have to be paid. When our house is sold, that will repay the mortgage and whatever is over will probably have to go back into the firm. I could teach music, which is what I'm qualified for. But where can I keep the piano? It has to be moved out of the house. There's no room big enough or suitable in the cottage." Marilyn leaned on the table, her face in her hands while the tears flowed. "I'm worthless. I feel there's no way out of this situation. Poor Howard."

"Now that's not correct. For one thing, you're not worthless, that fact is obvious to all who have known you, and can see you now. God says you are worthy, and Jesus loves you so much that He died to save you. You are precious. When we bring God into this situation He can change it in amazing ways. He has a plan for you both and it is for your good. He says so. I have experienced His work in my life, at times when I felt as you do. I believe that Jesus is working right now on your problems." Win paused and patted Mari's shoulder. "I can see that He brought us together today for that reason. I can recognise the way He arranges the circumstances. Looking back, we know that living is so difficult that we need God in our lives. He wants us to be with Him, and allow Him to guide and help us." Win hesitated and poured another glass of lemon while Mari watched her hungrily, the beginnings of hope in her eyes.

"How do you know this, Win? Have you seen this happening?"

"Yes indeed. I've made stupid mistakes. My life was a mess. You remember when you were at school, learning arithmetic, and you did a sum, but the answer didn't come out right? So you went to your teacher and she took you through the steps and showed where you went wrong? After that you could do it right, feeling good about it. God, in His power can make the crooked straight, and transform our lives while He's doing it."

Mari took a deep breath, saying, "Oh, if that were possible! It sounds too good to be true!"

"Yes, it is possible. A preacher told me how. The requirement is that I give up my pride and hand over my own life into Jesus' hands; giving Him full control; guiding me every day. I love Him now, knowing that He loves me so much."

Mari said, rather diffidently, "I see what He's done for you. I just wonder, seeing that He's so great in your life, why doesn't everyone in the world take Him into their lives?"

Win sighed. "That's the question with the sad answer. It's because our very first forebears, having been given freewill by God when He made them, were tempted by Satan and they disobeyed God's command. Satan was intensely proud. He said that he would be equal with God. Since then, everyone born is by nature a rebel against God."

They were silent for a few minutes. Birds cheeped through the seconds, while the bees continued to work on flowers in the sunshine.

"If Satan is a spirit, an evil spirit, he's invisible isn't he?" asked Mari.

"Yes he is."

"Can he put thoughts into our minds?"

"Yes, he can."

"Oh, that's light breaking in my mind!" said Marilyn. "It's thought battle, it's invisible. I've wondered how people, civilised people who knew how they ought to behave, can be so cruel, so selfish and greedy, starting wars and hurting people. Now I see, it's a battle while people think against God."

"Yes, and Satan teaches us to be proud."

"Is it pride that's behind a lot of our bad attitudes and wrong doing? Is that a name for sin?"

"Yes it is, at least it's behind very many sins." Mari's eyes had been fixed on Win's face as she talked. Now, Mari broke into a delighted smile. "At last I understand! This is all over the world. I know now why the world is so awful."

Win herself was beaming with pleasure at Mari's words. "I've said you were my favourite pupil. That's true now. I'm sure that God is pleased with your determination to learn. He loves you so much. You are His precious child." They paused, watching a few bees close by, as the shade of a tree moved nearer."

"Busy little workers aren't they?" said Mari. "Reminding me that

I should be home working. But this, this is so important, knowing what God is doing. It's satisfying. I'll never forget it, Win dear. Thank you so much."

"It's my pleasure, dear. Now, can I help you a little more? Have you a Bible? May I lend you one?"

"Yes, and thank you for that. Most of our books are packed."

"I thought as much. I'm suggesting a few verses which will help your faith. We all need help at such times as you are going through. Please ring me at any time, any day for that same reason. We can support one another in the battle. Jesus says that we are His family."

Marilyn nodded, holding the Bible and a list. "Thank you for lunch, and everything. You've made a difference in my life."

"Shall we have a little prayer before you leave? What's at the top of your list of needs?"

"Oh, so many things; the piano; somewhere to keep it and use it to teach. That would help."

"So that's how we'll pray. Lord God, we thank you for your love and the gift of your Son, Jesus. We bring this need to your attention and thank you for the answer. In Jesus' Name." They stood and while Mari gathered her things Win asked, "Now, are you all right? Can I deliver your load for you?"

"No, I'll be fine, thank you."

"We'll see each other again soon. Good bye my love." They hugged in mutual affection.

When she arrived home Mari approached the tasks awaiting her as some way she could bless people instead of being selfish or sad. She would ring her sons and ask them to take what they wanted to keep, or sell or re-home the rest. It would be satisfying to give to people who would appreciate it, or to op shops or social services. And so, asking God for help she tackled the job and had some progress to report to Howard when he arrived home. He also would have to decide what furniture he wanted to keep, and which of the multitude of his belongings likewise. His mood became relaxed at Mari's words. It seemed that the work day had passed with no particular crises. Howard's method of consulting each day with his managers kept the work going smoothly. Mari thanked God silently as they got on with the task of sorting their belongings.

The next morning, soon after Howard's departure, Marilyn's phone rang. It was Win's pleasant voice, now lifted with happiness. "Marilyn, I have news for you. I think I've found a home for your piano."

"Oh, wonderful, so soon! Tell me."

"Your previous teacher, Mrs Wakelin, is an old friend of mine. She remembers you and thinks highly of you and wants to help. She says she is slowing down and would like to cut her number of pupils. In fact, you are welcome to have your piano in her house, and take over some of her pupils. Would you like to do that?"

"Would I? I can hardly believe this offer! To be handed this on a plate! Thank you, thank you dear Winifred."

"You remember, we did ask the Lord. We can rely on Him, if you have committed yourself in your heart. He is gracious, and He is the one we have to thank."

"It's true, I did pray to Him last night. I'd be silly not to, thinking of the mess we're in."

"I agree with that sentiment. It was He who put the thought into my mind."

Chapter Three

S aturday dawned, and Gordon and Howard pooled their resources of tools, paint, sandpaper and brushes. Mari also came to help paint. While the men were hammering they were visited by a man who lived along the road.

"Gooday," he said. "My name's Jake. I heard you guys working and I'm offering to help. I'm a builder."

Both men shook his hand gratefully. Howard said, "That's kind of you. We can surely do with some skilled help. We're obviously not, so we'd appreciate your advice as well. I'm Howard Alton, this is my son Gordon."

"Pleased to meet you," said Gordon. "I'm only a school teacher. We do need help and good advice."

Mari approached and also shook his horny hand. She gave her best smile and said, "I'm Mari, the wife. You know how wives run up expenses for their husbands."

"They all do that," he said. "My wife's no exception. You'll meet her sometime." He produced his own hammer, looked at the house and said, "Tell me, what are you aiming to do here?"

Explanations followed and they set to work amicably. At midday they stopped for lunch.

"Stay, Jake," said Howard.

"Thanks, but my wife will have mine ready. I'll be back soon." When he returned he carried a damp bottle of beer, straight from the fridge. "Guess you haven't got a fridge here yet. Got a cool place to put it, Mari?"

"Oh, that's beaut." She aimed to match his speech. "I'll wrap it in a wet towel."

At the end of the afternoon they returned home, the Altons very tired with the unaccustomed work but some satisfaction. They found Tracy had cooked a good meal, and the children came running to meet them.

"This is so wonderful of you," said Mari, almost crying. "Bless you, Tracy. I'm so tired I'm ready to drop."

"Well, drop onto a chair. I can guess how you feel."

"Grandma, can we come again to your beach house?" asked Danny hopefully.

"Yes dear, of course. You can come lots of days. We're working there now so it will be nicer soon when you do come." She kissed his bright eyed face.

"Do sit down, everyone," said Tracy. "This is ready to eat." While they enthusiastically used knives and forks, the men answered Tracy's questions about progress.

"A good day's work and fine, thank goodness. A man who lives along the road, a builder came and offered his help. Jake, a very decent guy. He's probably got heaps of his own work to do. Even brought a chilled bottle of beer. It helped."

"Now, that's what I call a good neighbour. Soon, I hope you'll have your own fridge there and stock a bottle or two for when he drops in."

"Yes," said Mari, "a good idea. But I notice our own friends haven't dropped in or offered to help."

"That's the world for you," agreed Tracy. Mari thought back to her conversation with Win. "There are some good people. I told you that Win has found a home for my piano, with Mrs Wakelin, my old music teacher. She's even offering me a few of her pupils.

Her generosity is phenomenal. She could well be fed up with a string of kids coming into her house. We're in luck!"

She smiled at her husband who was still busy with his cutlery. "And Tracy and Gordon."

"Fair enough," said Gordon. "You helped us to get into our house. That was a big item."

"True. The first payment is hard to find. I'm glad I could do it back then," said Howard. "Soon, I hope, we can begin to move in. Though there's more work yet and it's very dirty inside. I hope you can manage it, Mari." She met his gaze with a nod.

"Yes. I know I've had it soft until now."

"I'll come over one morning and help you." Tracy was quick to offer.

"That's so generous of you, darling. You have your own house and the children."

"I'll help," offered Danny.

"Bless you, sweetheart. Yes, you shall come if you want to." Mari felt a lift in her spirit. After tidying the kitchen, bed was the most desirable place to be, and they slept soundly after their hard day.

On Sunday Howard was up early and brought coffee to a sleepy Marilyn. "Another fine day, so let's make the most of it."

"Mmm. I could have slept for a week after yesterday." She sat up reluctantly. "Look at my hands! Sandpaper doesn't agree with them. They hurt."

"We'll find you some gloves today. Come to think of it, my hands are a bit sore. A hammer can do lot of damage. I'll be pleased to be in an office tomorrow." He gazed at his wife fondly, as beautiful as ever, in spite of being tousled and tired, with a few lines at her eyes. "I'll make sure you have the car on the days you'll be teaching. Can't have the music teacher arriving on her bicycle all windblown and sweaty. We'll manage that somehow."

She looked at him with love, thankful that he looked more relaxed today. "Thank you darling. That will make life easier." She swung her legs out of bed and kissed him while finding her clothes.

"You're doing well, sweetheart," said Howard. "You're keeping me sane."

Downstairs, Mari hastily made sandwiches and filled a thermos with coffee. A detour to the shop, and again they met Gordon at the beach cottage. They surveyed the results with some self congratulations. "Not bad for amateurs," said Howard. "Jake's a great help isn't he?"

"Certainly is," said Gordon. "I'm learning skills, with his tricks of the trade."

"Me too," said Mari. "Perhaps I can hire myself out."

"You're an expert on the piano. That's a more ladylike job and kinder to your hands." They set to work, enjoying the breeze from the sea as it mixed with the clean smell of paint. At a brief mid-morning stop, Howard said, "I hope we can plan to move in soon. A bit more work; but I don't know what to do about that spouting. If we have a deluge... I'd like to ask Jake when I see him."

"I hope they're all having a good day away somewhere," said Mari. "He's so generous to help us after he works all week." She picked up her paint brush again, ignoring the desire to sit and rest. Her muscles were tiring, and she prayed silently, Lord help me to keep going.

It was a relief when midday came and she could call to the men, "Lunch time!" They were sitting on the floor to shelter from the sun, almost finished, when Jake appeared, wearing shorts and holding his hammer. His tall muscular body almost filled the doorway. They hailed him with delight, and Harvey leaped to his feet to shake his hand.

"Good to see you, mate."

"Couldn't make it earlier, sorry. I didn't want the kids to miss

Sunday school, so we all went to church." Mari felt a thread of hope restored.

"I remember I had a lovely Sunday school teacher when I was a kid," she said quietly. Jake gave a quick glance in her direction, with his slow smile. Howard hadn't noticed her words for he was so anxious to ask questions.

"Look at this, Jake. Do you think that should be removed and replaced? Or could we leave it for the time being?"

"Well that depends on how far ahead your plans go. It's all right for the short term. You know, just thinking of what would help you immediately; you could do well if you got your whole floor sanded now, and varnished before you move in. It's nice wood. It'll come up well."

"What a marvellous idea," said Howard. "I could send a man down to sand it on a work day."

"Excellent. I'll come in and varnish it, two coats before next weekend," said Jake. "You'd like to move into it, cleared of that dirt and the scuff marks, wouldn't you?" His gaze travelled round the group to Mari.

She burst in delightedly; "Yes please, it will make such a difference."

They all agreed with her.

"I'll buy the varnish and bring it if you tell me what sort," said Howard.

Mari went back to her painting, ridiculously happy and laughing silently at herself. What a thing to get excited about, a floor varnished. How I've changed. I'll enjoy telling Win about this kind man.

In early evening light they returned home just as tired as the previous night, but heartened by Jake's praise, "For a set of amateurs you've done well", also by his promise to varnish the floor. Tracy again cooked for them, echoing Howard's words, "I'm glad

I could do it." Mari's thoughts were about their beach neighbours, and hoping to repay their kindness sometime. None of their previous friends had sought them out.

Soon after breakfast on Monday, Mari hastened to ring her friend. "Win dear, we've had a great weekend. I'm sure God is with us, and He's sent Jake to help and advise us. It seemed such an impossible job, but Jake's a builder and has given us so much of his precious time. Gordon's a wonderful helper and Tracy too. I felt it was nearly going to kill me to get that place livable in a short time, but I think that with Jake offering to varnish the floors it will be much sooner. When they are sanded they'll look beautiful. It would have taken me a month to clean them."

"Truly, God is helping you, and precious Jake is an example of a friend going the second mile, as Jesus has told us to do. What a Christ-like act."

"That's right, and he had been taking his children to church on Sunday morning. I'm thrilled to think we'll have good neighbours. I guess you've been praying for us."

"Of course. That's the intelligent thing to do. He works with us because He loves us."

"I certainly need the Lord's help, to get through this week. More packing to do as well as keeping this house clean. And, most important, piano practice. My fingers are like wood. My hands need at least two hours a day, if I'm teaching. Dare I ask Tracy for more help?"

"Yes, at least for one or two days. She has offered. But, I'm happy to help you, today or any day. It will be my pleasure."

"Thank you, dear Winifred. I'd like to advertise very soon. Remember also, that when we move furniture, I'll be separated from my piano. It won't work to leave preparation for the future."

"I do see that. You are torn in many ways. The piano is the means of earning money. So, for today, I am yours and I'm happy to work and listen to the piano. Believe me. I'll see you soon."

Half an hour later Tracy arrived without being asked, with Melissa and a few toys. "She'll amuse herself for a couple of hours with these," said Tracy. "It's only what she would be doing at home. It's not like having lively Danny here, poking into everything. Now, what are we doing first?" Mari was sitting cuddling Melissa, and reluctantly put her down.

"Linen cupboards, kitchen cupboards, packing the necessary things for the cottage, which will mean not very much. I expect we'll be more or less camping for who knows how long. I'm almost resigned to the thought of living rough forever. Tracy dear, if you see anything you'd like to keep or have a long loan of, please take it."

"Well, perhaps a long loan, but certainly I can store things for you. You won't be exiled forever, and not too long at that, I'm sure. There will be times when you'll want to dig into boxes for this or that."

"I'm thankful that you are so comforting, and practical. Oh, there's someone at the door. Probably Winifred." A moment later, Mari ushered Win into the room, saying,"Tracy, meet a very special friend. This is my childhood mentor, much loved and now my present mentor, Mrs Meldrum."

"Call me Winnie. I'm delighted to meet you, Tracy, and this beautiful little girl. You are indeed blessed, Mari."

"I know that," said Mari. "You've yet to meet Danny, who's now at kindy. He's so lively, I don't know how Tracy copes."

"I'm so pleased that you are helping Mari. She doesn't deserve this earthquake in her life," said Tracy. "It's wonderful to have your help."

"Many hands, you know," said Mari, "to fill many boxes; a couple to take the minimum of necessities to the beach house, as I've listed; some to dump or possibly sell, boxes to store for better days."

"I can offer you storage space," said Win, "for medium or even short term storage. You may find you'll need to dip into it, occasionally."

"That would be wonderful. You never know what might happen. There's simply no room; it will be like camping."

"I know. Now, as your mentor, I hear that piano calling you. We two can get to know each other. It will be pleasant."

"That's a weight off my mind. I also need to ring a few people who will take some things off my hands," said Mari lightly, leaving them.

Time passed quickly. Tracy put her head in to say good bye as she left to pick up Danny. Mari went to the kitchen to put a small lunch together.

Win joined her, saying, "I do like your daughter-in-law. I hope you're feeling satisfied with your hard work. I can hear that it's not easy to pick up skill after a break of years."

"You're right there. I know I can't do it in a day. But, thanks to you I've made a start. Tomorrow and the next day I'll improve."

As they sat at the kitchen table eating their lunch, Win said, "I've an idea which just might help you. Have you a satisfactory kitchen arrangement in the beach house? I know it's often lacking in a holiday batch."

"Yes, you could say that. There's a sink and a stove, that's all."

"Well, what do you think about buying a cheap wooden bench for storing your basic kitchen stuff and to work on. Not elegant but cheap and adequate. Would you and your husband like to look in the builders' supplies shop or a second hand place?"

"What a good idea! Lead me there, today, you and me. I can tell Howard if I see anything I like. I'm sure he'll be pleased if I find something to help us. We'll know then where to place the power points. I'll tell him tonight."

When Howard arrived home that evening he saw a collection of boxes and crates, all labelled. "You have been busy," he said.

"Yes," said Mari. "I've had two helpers, Tracy and Mrs Meldrum, my Sunday school teacher. What's more, because they know it's urgent for me to exercise my hands before I get back to teaching, they gave me two hours of time to practise while they packed and sorted."

"I didn't know you had to practise. I thought you just played the piano."

She kissed him. "You're lucky if you think that's all there is to it. Hands, arms, brains, all muscles to be strengthened. If I don't it shows, and I ought not to try to teach. I have to be professional."

"I see. So you get paid."

"That's right. Now sit down, this dinner's ready to eat." Mari served two portions of steak. "Serve yourself to salad. How was your day?"

"Really busy. We aim at being professional too and the day has gone well. Good steak. I'm glad you could pay the butcher."

"I could guess that you're gaining respect; Cobbles absent, and you're trying very hard to make things run well. Could you call it running a tight ship?"

"It certainly feels like work, keeping the standards high. I've no spare time in the day. I suppose he and I were more relaxed at times, and possibly wasted time here and there. I don't like to think how he spent his time."

"Hmm. Very nasty thought. Anyway, now you're home, I hope you'll sort through your things, pack stuff for storage, think what to sell. Like golf clubs; and decide what to bless someone else with."

"True. I know we've accumulated things we haven't needed. We can make the op shops happy."

"Talking about the butcher, I've sold some bits of jewellery. I feel I've been spoilt until now and I want to pull my weight. Good stones and gold are like money in the bank, I've found, and you've invested in me for this present time. Winifred told me how to improve the functioning of the cottage. So, today, I put a deposit on a wooden bench with shelves, to make my kitchen workable, and if you approve we could pick it up when we're ready to move in."

"What a clever girl you are. I didn't know I had married such a talented lady. There's a lot behind that pretty face." He came round the table and kissed her. "If I've spent money on you it's well spent. Consider yourself part of the business." He paused. "I don't suppose you've measured this piece of furniture?"

"Of course I have. Here you are." She showed him the diagram. He studied it.

"Excellent. That music school trained you well. I'll give this to the electrician; we need plenty of power points. Soon we'll be ready to move in. You're worthy of a raise."

"When?" She swatted him on the head with a tea towel.

"Next year. Remind me."

Next day the land agent phoned to arrange an appointment at the house. Two men sat at a table with Howard and Mari, making notes. She tried to concentrate on the job in hand, and not to think that this was the end of her world.

"We're advertising by computer as well as in the other cities, to whip up interest. It's worth a little extra trouble for such a handsome package. We think auction is best for this case. Now, did you say that you may sell some furniture, specific pieces, with the house?"

"Yes, that's right, especially the Queen Anne bedroom suite, six pieces in the main bedroom. It's solid mahogany, hand carved. The lounge suite is new, four pieces which match the carpet and curtains, also. Could we call those a separate sale, by negotiation?"

"We'll make a note of that. Anything else? Give us a price for each room."

"Let's walk about and look. I don't want any pieces of furniture included as part of the price of the house," said Mari.

They discussed and made notes as they walked. Mari said, "This guest room has a rather nice set of furniture, pretty wood, including two matching bed side tables. It was somewhat of a luxury when we bought it. I'd be happy to sell it."

"When do you think the auction will be?" asked Howard.

"We have in mind two weeks from today. If it suits you to move out with what you need, the good stuff you leave will build up the attraction."

"So long as they know that it's a separate sale, I'm happy," said Mari.

"We're in agreement then. Tell us your lawyers." The agents left with their photos and clip-boards.

"Phew. We've done it. Now I'll go back to work to make some more money. I've had a quite good offer for the big car. That should help, short term."

"That's a relief. We can't avoid day to day expenses." After Howard returned to work, Mari drifted towards the kitchen, thinking some coffee might relieve her feeling of emptiness. She didn't know what to do next. This is not my house any more. I'm being torn out of it. My heart is bleeding, after loving every minute of living here. With a mug of coffee in her hand, tears on her face , she stumbled to pick up her phone. Dialing Win's number was an act of desperation. Win's soft voice answered; thank heavens for that.

"Dear Win, I think I'm falling apart. The house is sold, well nearly. I feel wounded and I don't know how to carry on. I just want to die."

"Hold on, darling girl. I'm coming. I'll be with you in ten minutes. Stay put there."

Mari sat in a gray haze of grief. Time passed. Then she heard the sound of a car. Mari was drawn to the door. They hugged, wordless.

It's like my mother being here, thought Marilyn thankfully. She didn't want to let go.

"Dear child," said Win gently. "Can we sit out here in the sun? Take the weight off our feet? That's better, isn't it. I see your world is falling apart; one thing after another. The shocks, the death, the robbery. Now your house is going. Did you have the land agents here today?" Mari nodded. "The final blow. Your husband still has his work, same surroundings. But most of your friends have vanished, and you fear the gossip, or what may be said of you in your changing circumstances. Words can hurt, can't they? The world has let you down." Win touched Mari's shoulder sympathetically.

Mari wiped her eyes. She said, "This house and the lovely garden and trees; it's been beautiful living here. Some of that entertaining wasn't enjoyable, or not to me. But after people had gone away my house and my beautiful trees always comforted me. I thought it must have been made for us. For our future."

"But you know, we shall be having a different future, a special one that God has planned for us. We hope and dream up for ourselves a bright and happy one, not understanding God's plans. We won't know until we're there. Jesus said, 'In My Father's house are many dwelling places. If it were not so I would have told you; for I am going away to prepare a place for you. There, I will receive you unto Myself, that where I am , you will be also.'" Win studied Mari's face, to note her reaction. She was absorbed, concentrating on the words but with no more tears. "You have received several shattering blows in a short time. Jesus, Son of God, is the Person who can heal you by giving an enormous gift lasting forever. If you are willing to receive it you can be healed as He will inhabit your mind and your body. Giving yourself as an empty cup for Him to fill is the secret."

"But can He change these difficult, unpleasant things that are in front of me now?" asked Mari, her face crumpling in grief.

"Yes, but not by taking them away. With Jesus' Spirit indwelling you, you will see them differently because He is in your eyes. He sees the result, He strengthens your mind and your body to tackle the actions, the work and the endurance to complete it. Do you believe that He loves you, not a little but to an astounding degree?"

"If you tell me, I can believe it."

"Do you love him enough to give Him control of your life?"

"Yes, if that means taking me to be with Himself for always in the place He prepares."

"That's why Jesus died on the cross, carrying our sins, so that we, redeemed by His sacrifice could become sons and daughters of God, cleansed, then purified by God, to become fit people to live with Jesus, in pure harmony, in the place He is preparing for us."

"If that means what I suppose it means, a place to call Heaven, in eternity, well yes I would love to be filled with His Spirit. I love Him heaps."

Win prayed, "Our precious Lord, Jesus Christ, we believe that you are here with us, as you love us. I ask that you are now filling Marilyn with your Spirit, to comfort and heal her. And that will be forever more. I ask in Jesus' Name. Amen."

They sat silently for a couple of minutes. Marilyn was breathing deeply and calmly. Then she said "This is important, isn't it? I believe He's done it."

"Bless you, darling. I'm sure He has. He loves you so much, He'll never let you down. When we put him in control of our life, He is absolutely reliable."

"Thank you," said Mari. "I feel I can carry on now with my work. And I must put in piano practice."

"Now that I'm here, I may as well help you for a couple of hours. You just find me a job to do, right now, while you go to the piano. I'll enjoy hearing you."

"Playing scales! Not exciting, but I accept your offer because it'll ease my mind." Much relieved, Mari worked on her dull exercises until she called a break. "That's better," she said. "Time for coffee and a nibble in the kitchen. This really is helping. I've improved since yesterday. I feel better now, I know everything is in control."

"Yes, I know Jesus is able to enhance our performance, piano or whatever it is. He's an ever-present help when we ask Him to be."

"Like you do. I'm so glad we met that day."

"Good morning, Winifred, I'm just about bursting to talk to you."

"It's lovely to hear you, Mari. How are you today?"

"I feel wonderful, really full of joy. I'm happy and able to work. There's something inside me that's bubbling up. I love it, I love Him. When I woke up and looked out this morning it was all so beautiful, I couldn't help saying "Thank you God." Of course this garden's always exquisite, but today it's more so, and even though I have to leave it I know the next garden will be equally so. Howard is very surprised by me, and asks me what's happened. I don't know how to explain. He might think I'm mad. If I am, I hope it lasts a long time. I feel full to over-flowing with love for nearly everyone, and peaceful. My mind is somehow richer and I now have answers to things I never thought about before. Don't think I'm boasting, but that's how I feel. Have you ever been like this, Win?"

"Yes, my dear. I can guess exactly how you feel. You are experiencing what some call the honeymoon, when one is newly filled with Jesus' Holy Spirit. He is a gentleman who waits to be asked, and you have invited Him in. You are able to keep this awareness of His Spirit for the rest of your life, as long as you continue to maintain your relationship with Him. God is love, actually love. That's how He manages to love the unlovable of this world."

"Can I keep this for always? Do you have this happiness, Win?"

"Yes, Mari, I do. And I want to explain something to you. Sometimes we can lose the happiness part, as when bad illness or the evil one attacks our brain. But there is a quiet joy deep down, in our innermost being, as the Bible tells us. But we know it deeply, and no one or any circumstance can take it from us. We continue to relate to Jesus. He wants us to. That's what it really means to be a Christian."

"Is that how some people lived, people who died as martyrs?"

"Yes. In the times of persecution of Christians, they would have known that to persist in living as believers would have meant imprisonment or death, their deep faith and love for God was stronger than fear of what men could do."

"I think I know now how they would be feeling. But I have never been through that sort of trial."

"They, filled by the Holy Spirit, would have a supernatural strength. I think you've had a taste of that this morning. I expect you will continue to experience His strength, if you keep on praying and thanking Him. It's an amazing fact that God, great though He is, wants so much to have our love and a really close relationship with us. We don't know why. But He made us, with that in His mind. As we live, we can see that He is allowing us to have trials which may help us to become beautiful people, fit and desirable to live with for Jesus to have as companions all through eternity."

"Thinking about that, I can see that not too many people could fit into that category. Yes, it's a great aim. I hope I make the grade."

"Keep on praying and trusting Him, reading the scriptures, making your heart absolutely honest with Him. He is always reading our hearts. We can't fool God. If you remember what we talked about in our lessons so long ago, about the Pharisees."

"I think so. Were they horrible men, proud and unloving? Jesus called them appalling names. He could read their hearts."

"That's right. I've always called you my favourite pupil because you remember important, basic facts."

"Win, don't praise me and make me swell-headed, because

I might believe you and then become one of those unpleasant Pharisees."

"I'm saying that because you are pleasing God. He says that He wants us to pursue Him, to use our intelligence to spend time, in learning and thinking about all He has done for us, and appreciate Him. We love him for Himself."

"I can see that, as you love me and help me, so it is with God."

"Bless you, Marilyn, you are truly a daughter of God."

Chapter Four

The following days of that week were full of to-and-fro. The gardener was present most days engaged in mowing, trimming and weeding; phones and door bells were ringing. Many difficult decisions were made. Marilyn's moods varied between frenetic activity and heartache (this is the last time I'll see this). Midway through the day, as the door closed behind one visitor, she stood numbly, fingers on her temples. She felt lost. But her gratitude for her relationship with the Holy Spirit was under and over all that was happening. She schooled her thoughts to touch again that precious awareness that remained deeply in her brain. At times she calmed herself by spending time on the piano. This was effective too. Better days lay ahead, she told herself.

A multiplicity of crates and cartons grew near both doors. Gordon, father of two, was the one who packed toys and games, thinking of the future of the grandchildren. Mari's heartache was salved by these actions; she could look forward to the children enjoying what she and Harvey had accumulated. Tracy became Mari's right hand, always doing whatever was needed. She transported many items of Mari's evening clothes to her friend in another city. Harvey tidied his big desk which was to be fitted into the cottage, albeit with difficulty.

Rodney came rather petulantly to pick up his clothes and chattels which, to him were important. He told his mother to dump the rest, leaving her with the task of finding recipients who would be grateful to accept the luxurious belongings of an indulged young man. Only Sylvia was still away, with her architect husband Ben, at present in Israel with Ben's father. Ben was using his prolonged honeymoon to look at buildings in several countries. But they were planning to return shortly, satiated with travel.

Mari was longing to see her much-loved daughter, who was gifted in many ways like her mother, with a practical turn of mind as well. I wonder what she'll think about our straitened circumstances, about her mother becoming a bread-winner again; above all Mari's change of heart and contentment to live a much simpler life as a disciple of Jesus. Sylvia, always a naturally good dancer, had chosen to become a qualified teacher of physical culture.

So the week days flew, aiming at moving house the following week. Mari's life was fully disciplined, including piano practice. After all, I may have pupils next week. I have to put this house out of my mind and not look at the new season's growth in the garden. I won't be here to enjoy it. This is pain, as I've never experienced it before. But Jesus suffered far more than this, as have many people. Lord, be Lord of all things in my life. I know that you will never leave me nor forsake me. You, Lord, are in control.

At the day's end she walked wearily to her bed. Howard was already asleep. She pulled off her clothes and slid in beside him. A well-known line of music came into her mind; He, watching over Israel, slumbers not nor sleeps. That's God, she remembered; He slumbers not nor sleeps. With a smile on her own face she fell asleep.

In anticipation of moving day, Mari chose a bedroom suite of simple furniture to be taken to the cottage. They would put two single beds together. She urged Tracy to take some for her as-yet-empty spare bedroom, to which Tracy said, "As a loan, until you want to take it back. I can easily imagine a couple of grand kids thinking what fun it would be to spend the night with Grandma." That thought also had appeal.

The piano and boxes of music-associated books would travel to the house of kind, generous Mrs Wakelin. "I'll have to organise myself to cope with all this," Mari told herself. She had never before been separated from her piano.

Howard had also been careful with expenditure and, thankful to say, they were solvent. "I know what to do," he said. "I'll ask that second hand shop to deliver that kitchen bench to the cottage. They do that sort of thing. If you travel with them, Mari, you can show them the way. On Saturday we'll go down and tidy it up, probably it will need it. We'll have to have a bench to put things on. Moving day will be that much better."

Marilyn agreed gratefully. "Have we worked out what our address is?"

"As far as I remember, it's simply Beach Road. Do they have numbers? There are not many houses, and a lot of space. Let's ask the Post office. I'm glad I'm not the postman. Anyway, shall we book a van with two men for Monday ?"

"Tuesday I think. Have an extra day to prepare. I hope you'll have the day off work."

"Part of it. A few hours I expect. You'll be a good sergeant-major."

On Friday Mari and a van driver drove to Beach Road house. As Mari unlocked the door the pleasant smell of varnish met her, and to her delight she found the floor gleaming and clean; definitely a far more attractive sight than before. Thank you Jake, you're an angel, she thought. The driver manipulated the bench out of the van with only a little help from Mari. They slid it into place using skids to protect the floor. Stage one, thank you Lord. She had learned to take nothing for granted. I'll scrub it tomorrow, she decided.

Saturday morning was the time for finishing the painting and, for Mari, the scrubbing of the least inviting parts, the bathroom in particular. She used lots of disinfectant, hard brushes and scrapers, with gloves to protect her tender skin. While she worked, inwardly groaning about the unpleasant smells (yukky, yukky), and trying not to think about how many people had used this 'convenience' she began to feel sympathy for the many women who had worked like this for most of their lives; probably without complaint. I know I've been lucky, growing up with music and dance, and at times helping Mother in the kitchen. I'm like a hot house flower. It's time for me to grow up. With relief she decided that was all she could achieve today.

Joining the men, she said, "I've done what I can there. Do you think we could put a bit of paint on the worst bits?"

"Sure thing," answered Howard. "We'll do it last today, so it'll dry over night." He took a quick look. "You've done well. Smells better."

Mari turned to her purchase, the kitchen bench. With a good scrub of the top and shelves it could be practical if not beautiful. When lined up with the new power points it would be easy to use. Mentally thanking Win for her forethought, Mari realised how hopeless it would have been to move in with no bench. God is helping us, she affirmed, in all sorts of ways. Hopefully she could fit in some piano practice today. It's not long to moving day.

On Tuesday the sun smiled on them until it was lowering in the western sky, and touching the tips of the waves with silver. They sat enjoying this evening, six of them using four wooden chairs and two easy chairs, although Gordon then sat on the doorstep, facing the sea. The incoming tide lapped sweetly onto the beach. It was a time for rest, for the enjoyment of a day's work successfully completed, with the cooperation of all concerned.

"I never thought," said Mari, "that I could be as happy as this after what has happened."

"Mmm," said Tracy, her sleepy baby on her knees, "I'm so glad for you that it has worked out as well as it has."

"It's not too bad, is it?" said Howard. "Now my wife can keep her cold feet in her own bed."

Danny, also drooping with sleepiness on his wooden chair, said, "Grandma, can I sleep here tonight?"

"Sorry darling, just now I haven't a bed for you. But later, in a little while, I'll get a little bed specially for you to spend the night. Our space is so cramped, with Grandpa's big desk here. But I'll work out something, I promise."

"We'd better be on our way home to find your baths and beds," said Tracy.

"What a great day it's been," said Mari. "You two helping, Gordon after school, Winifred's big fat sandwiches for lunch, and Tracy's casserole tonight. You've made it so easy, bless you. We've so much to be thankful for; the fine weather, two helpful moving men to shift things. Before you came, Gordon, Jake's wife brought us fresh baked scones. Her name's Nellie."

"Good neighbours are a blessing to cultivate and hang onto," said Tracy. "Now I'll gather up dirty plates and dishes. I brought some so we wouldn't leave you work."

"You're a treasure, Tracy," said Howard. "We'll never forget all you and Gordon have done. Thanks for your loyalty." Unsaid in their thoughts were the names of some not present.

Gordon stood and began to gather up the plates. Danny slid down from his wooden chair, saying, "I'll get my crabs."

"Your CRABS!" squealed Tracy.

"They're in my bucket," said Danny, setting off.

Gordon took pity on Tracy, and said, "Danny, the crabs won't be happy if you take them to our house. They like living in the sea, they find their dinner in the sea. Don't you think it would be kind to put them back, and you'll find them next time we come here?"

"All right. I want them to be happy." He trotted down to the beach.

"You may have a budding scientist there, Tracy. You'll be proud of him one day," said Howard.

Their packing up completed, Gordon and Tracy drove off into the dusk, promising to come again soon.

Howard and Mari settled into the easy chairs, listening to the swishing of waves on the beach and the occasional calls of wading birds. "Are you okay now, Mari? You've coped better than I expected."

"Thank you. You've done famously too. Let's go out for a minute and enjoy our view."

They walked the few meters to the high tide level. After a minute Mari said, "Isn't it lovely? And we're here, no rent or mortgage to pay. When the house is sold and that mortgage is paid, well, please God, the worst of our troubles will be over."

"Then, I hope, our continued hard work will pay off."

Chapter Five

Marilyn woke slowly, aware of a different atmosphere, with sounds of the waves and sea gulls. It was a comfort to her mind to realise that this would be a secure life; that the Lord was now in control. She was being careful not to express these thoughts to Howard; not yet, anyway. Some people, she knew, could be 'put off' by Godly talk, sad to say. 'He is my shelter,' the words seemed to sing in her mind. Did I make that up, she wondered. I believe that was Jesus saying it. I must ask Win if that's a scripture. Thanks to Him we're safely housed. A few inadequacies in the building but outside we have the beauty of the sea, its mystery and charms, and its inhabitants which already had Danny enthralled. Silently she prayed and thanked the Lord, asking for His help in this day for herself and Howard. She glanced at him, apparently sleeping, and was reluctant to wake him. Last night he was very tired. As they kissed and slid into their respective beds, he had seemed somewhat relieved, she thought, and would need healing sleep.

Mari made a quick breakfast in their make-do kitchen, which they ate with the door open to enjoy the view and the sea breeze. Howard was cheerful and set off in the car with the packed lunch, handed to him while Mari kissed him. "Don't forget to eat it," she advised, knowing that pressure of work could cause him so to do. Now, what's urgent? she asked herself. I know I must contact Mrs

Wakelin and reach my piano, but our phone is not connected. I'm longing to look at my future garden though I can't put time into it yet. I think I'd better ask Nellie if I may use her phone first.

After a quick tidy of the dishes, and thankful for a good hot water service, she walked to her nearest neighbour. As expected, she was seeing her children off to school. Peter, Graham and Sarah were attractive, well-mannered children displaying the good traits of their parents. They departed at a trot, to connect with the school bus a little distance away.

"Hullo Nellie," said Mari. "I'm sorry I'm making a nuisance of myself already. Our phone's not yet connected, so may I use yours?"

"Of course, Mari," she said, her ready smile identifying her personality. She was slightly shorter than Mari, inclined to plumpness with a round face, dimples and bright brown eyes. "I'm very untidy at this time of day so don't look at me. It's pleasant to have you as a new neighbour."

"You might be surprised that we're moving into a tiny beach cottage, as though we're here permanently. There's reason for it though. My husband's business partner died suddenly, leaving us to find that he had been embezzling large chunks of the firm's money. And so, we have to sell our house quickly to put that money into the firm."

"Oh, poor you. What a dreadful thing to inflict on you!" Nellie's expressive face was sympathetic.

"So, as you can understand, we are tremendously grateful to your husband for helping us to make the place habitable. And for your welcome yesterday, well we are touched by your kindness. When experiencing trouble, you learn how precious good friends are."

"I can sympathise. We all have troubles at times. That is true, about friends."

"Indeed so. We thought we had lots of them, until the night of the party at our house. The partner died, next came the financial crash, and almost all the friends disappeared. Though we do have some older friends and they are being wonderful in their support."

"That's so good to hear. Well, there's the phone, use it all you please and welcome. You are definitely not a nuisance."

"Thank you," said Mari, and proceeded to phone Mrs Wakelin and her friend Winifred. To Nellie she said, "I'll be riding my bike today, to the home of the kind lady who is holding my piano. But on days when I shall be teaching, Howard will leave the car for me. As you'll understand, we had to sell the big car."

"I know, we've had that awkward situation too. Anytime I'm going into town I can take you too."

"That is gracious of you. However, today being fine I'm happy to bike. It will be good for my figure."

"You're an example to us all. Enjoy your day."

I'll try, thought Marilyn, but she had some trepidation. I'm no longer a teenager to cycle long distances, encountering strong wind. Kind Mrs Wakelin may regret the ongoing nature of my need. I could overuse my welcome. But I've no choice at this moment. Lord, please help me, she said as she leaned into the pedals for the slight rise. Words immediately sounded in her brain, 'I will never leave you.'

The pleasant weather made for a happy arrival at Mrs Wakelin's house. That lady welcomed her, smiling and saying, "My dear, how lovely to see you. You must be a little tired after your exertions."

"Thank you for your kindness, Mrs Wakelin," said Mari. She allowed herself to be led into the familiar room, with the glossy upright piano and comfortable deep armchairs. A table was set for morning tea.

"Tea or coffee, whichever you prefer. Now, make yourself at home. I'll pour your drink and let you refresh yourself. Sugar?"

The pleasant medium-old house was full of good memories for Mari, for she had enjoyed learning music. Mrs Wakelin was an excellent teacher, now become motherly. Mari relaxed in the atmosphere.

"Try these chocolate biscuits to restore your energy. You haven't lost your girlish good looks. You were always a joy to teach. I'm so pleased that you're continuing to put your gifts into helping young players. I'm told that you encourage those on the way up."

"You've been a wonderful teacher to me. I loved those years of learning and you've taught me discipline. I would have failed the exams if you had not."

"You have a lot of character, Marilyn. Winifred tells me that you're coping well with a patch of bad luck."

"It's true, we are struggling through a very difficult situation. Mr Cobbold died suddenly in what was supposed to be a celebration party; a ghastly descent into the opposite."

"I see. I used to know them slightly, and I heard a lot more, none of it good. And your husband was in partnership with him. Oh dear, one does hear rumours, though it's hard to know what to believe. But I am pleased to be able to make life a little easier for you. And, you know, I have wanted for quite a while to retire from teaching, but not completely. This way, in touch with you, I feel I have the best of both worlds. Now, let me show you how I've placed your piano." She led Mari to her spare bedroom, a pleasant size with pale green walls and the piano, with its stool and boxes of books. "See, good lighting, plugs for heaters, privacy if you shut the door, or open as you please."

"Ooh, it's perfect! I couldn't ask for more. Thank you so much, dear Mrs Wakelin." And Mari couldn't resist giving her a quick hug. But that lady was smiling at this demonstration.

"I'm so glad I can help you. I'll give you a list, names of my pupils, and you may choose how many and when. I have found that many of them find Saturday suits them. These are the grades beside their names. We can talk about them when you've had time to think."

So Mari sat and practised with contentment, considering her partnership with her hostess.

Marilyn's next appointment was with her friend Winifred, an invitation to lunch. As she expected, the welcome was indeed very warm. "Dear Win, I feel so grateful for all this kindness, I'm almost crying. Mrs Wakelin is so very generous, it's unbelievable. God is surely helping us."

"He is surely our source of supply when we put all our trust in Him. And He throws in all sorts of blessings to encourage us. So how was your first night at the beach?"

"Beautiful. It makes me think that God was urging me to like that place so that when our troubles started we would have a refuge waiting for us. Danny loves the sea creatures so much, we think that he might become a scientist. But Tracy doesn't want them in her house. I'm wondering how we might be able accommodate his needs."

"There speaks a generous Grandma. But being next door to the sea he shouldn't have a problem. Only, you'll have a permanent boarder. You must be hungry, my dear. Come to the table. Do you like fish pie? You do. It's a nourishing meal for a hard working girl."

They settled to eat. First hunger satisfied, Winifred continued to press for details of Mari's new expectations, which she was happy to share, knowing Win's reasons. "Now I gather you've been with Mrs Wakelin today. How did that go?"

"She likes the thought of sharing pupils in her house. We get on well. She wants to partly retire, but still be at the heart of the music world. She's wonderfully kind in the way she has arranged privacy and comfort for me. We have yet to discuss names and details of the students. I may speak to some before Saturday."

"You will make a good team. God has gone before you. I can see the signs of His work."

"I can see that too. I'm so thankful about the way things have worked out. I love Him heaps and heaps. Perhaps we can reach children who might otherwise miss out. The study of music develops the function of the brain and that's always good, and gives confidence."

"An excellent aim, to help more children to learn and enjoy making music. You'll make long term friends, and enrich their lives."

"I hope so. I know I've been lucky."

"Would you like to tell me your plans for this, your new first week? Then I'll know how to pray for you. I'm concerned about the extra effort in getting about by bicycle."

"Today was all right, in fine weather. The extra distance takes more time, of course, and I'm learning to hide my pride in my pocket. It's good exercise, therefore healthy for me. Howard wants me to have the car on my teaching days, when he'll make other arrangements."

"And so, we'll ask the Lord to keep you safe, and supply all your needs. I know He will, and you are welcome to ask me for help in travel. I love to help you. In fact, today, I guess you may be heading for your big house, to make things ready for the sale."

"Yes, I have to pack some things and clean here and there."

"Mari, I ought to make this day easier for you. You have a very long day, with all this biking. I think it's right for me to help you. Let me drive you to your big house and help you pack or clean, whatever you're doing. Then we come back here for your ride home. It's hard work and difficult."

"Thank you, dear Winifred. I appreciate that so much. Yes, the sale day will be next week."

"I know how topsy-turvy one feels in the middle of shifting. It's emotionally draining."

Mari was tired as she cycled home in the late afternoon. But going downhill was easy and it was a relief to be making progress. When Howard arrived home she had his meal ready and he appreciated how well she had coped with her day. It was certainly a pleasure to be close to the sea, almost like being on holiday, as Mari said.

"So you were right in choosing this cottage by the beach," said Howard.

"I know I was. Just ask Danny."

The next morning was notable for the fact that an employee of the telephone company arrived to make their connection. "You are so welcome," said Mari. "Here please, by my husband's desk. Thank you very much."

She celebrated by phoning Winifred. "I'm so pleased that now I can bother you more often. I don't mind if you regret it and cut me off sometimes."

"Of course I'm pleased for you. You know that you are a special person to me. What are you planning for today?"

"Mainly, I guess, I prepare for these pupils, their progress, and what they are working on. I hope to please them, and that they won't mind changing teacher. Practise and make notes and talk to Mrs Wakelin about them."

"Will you be able to come for lunch, and allow us to have prayer time? There are so many important items happening now. Your house sale for one."

"Yes, I'm aware of that. Next week, then Sylvia's return. Some important talking will take place."

"Come in, my dear. Your pupils are fortunate to have you preparing so well. I'm sure they'll love you for it."

"I hope so. It's years since I did any teaching, so I'm a little nervous. This is a lovely meal, and in your company it's very pleasant."

Soon, appetites satisfied, they mentioned the upcoming events.

"We're hoping for a really good result of this auction to cover our mortgage and more, to build up the firm's finances," said Mari.

"That's how we'll pray then. Dear Lord, we praise you and love you, we bless your presence in our lives. You know these circumstances, and that Howard does not want to put any of his staff off. He wants to be a good employer, and honest in everything he does. So we ask you Lord, for a fine day for this auction and good work by the land agents and their contacts about the country. May there plenty of rich clients to lift the selling price of this beautiful house and garden. In your kindness and love, Jesus, and may you be glorified in this piece of business."

"Thank you, God, we are depending on you for continuing high quality of work in the firm, and healthy finances for all the staff and their families. In Jesus' name."

"Our heavenly Father, we thank you for your loving kindness and daily support. In your mercy we put our trust. I ask you Lord, to help Mari in her work, and the family relationships. May they all come to know and love you, and to be witnesses for you and learn to praise your Name, Jesus. To you be the glory."

Saturday came, and Marilyn was tingling with excitement. She drove the car in comfort, and was thankful for it. She had learned now, not to take anything for granted. Mrs Wakelin, very graciously, introduced each pupil as she arrived, telling them that the new teacher was a highly qualified person, and had her personal recommendation. The response was good, and the morning passed very pleasantly. At midday Mari drove to Winifred's house, sure of her welcome there.

"Come in, my dear, I've been looking forward to this."

"Thank you, Win. This is such a pleasant break for me."

"Lunch is on the table. Come and help yourself when you're comfortable."

"It looks delicious. Green salad with eggs in dressing and tomatoes. They're early." She took a few mouthfuls.

"Now, when you've eaten, tell me how was your morning?"

"Very good over all. They seemed to accept me and we could get on, as well as one could wish. These are younger pupils, and Mrs Wakelin did as she had planned, introducing me instead of me ringing them first. It was the best way, although, for the older teenagers it might be well for me to speak first, in case, being almost adults, they want to choose. I don't want to tread on any toes."

Win's bright attention was on Mari's face. "That's a sensitive way of thinking on your part."

"The children responded to me very well. I know how to praise while giving them suggestions. I smiled and so did they. When I said, see you next Saturday, they appeared to be happy."

"I knew you would be likable and a good teacher. Were there hiccups?"

Mari laughed a little as she sliced an egg. " Well, it happens that one little girl is the daughter of a couple who used to be in our crowd of so-called friends. I haven't seen them since that disastrous night of the party. They probably would cut me dead if we met in the street. The kid doesn't know me but I recognise the surname. And when she tells her ma about her new teacher, I expect my name will be mud; anything could happen."

There was a pregnant pause. "You're a highly qualified musician and teacher. She can't deny that. I suggest you do nothing but go on being a good teacher. This girl will probably like you. What's her name."

"Augusta."

"O-gusta! Oh la la! They are ambitious. I hope she's not spoilt."

"Quite likely is. But I can lay onto her the need for strict standards and discipline. After that, it's up to them."

"I hope she makes the most of your good teaching. You will have more pupils today?"

"Yes, several more, including twin boys. They will be interesting.

Now I must start back, again thanking the Lord for His help. I'm sure He is helping me."

Feeling a little tired but relaxed and happy, Mari drove towards home. She was surprised to see a car parked outside. Who can that be, she wondered. Oh, amazing, it's Rodney! Haven't seen him for weeks. I hope he's not being difficult. But when she parked she heard voices outside, then, investigating, found him at the back, working with Howard.

Two tall men, both in shorts, were handling planks of wood. They turned at her arrival, and Mari ran to Rodney and hugged him then turned to her husband and kissed him. Rodney looked a little embarrassed, while Howard explained, "Rod rang and offered to help me, so here we are attempting to build a shelter for the car. We think the previous owner might have had some such here, and left some bits of wood lying here."

"That's wonderful!" said Mari. "I had noticed some wood lying here. Do you know how, or has Jake helped you?"

"We don't really know how, but a little talk with Jake gave us some idea how to get started. We went in Rod's car and bought a bit more. I think Rod's showing some talent."

"I'm sure you have talent, Rod. As a little boy you liked tools."

"Thanks Mum," he grinned. "How was your day? Dad says you are teaching again."

"I've had a good day, getting to know my pupils. An interesting set of children. Now I'll go and make your dinner, after I've put my feet up for ten minutes."

Mari thankfully sat in a comfortable chair, listening to the sea on the beach, with a heart full of gratitude. Lord, you are amazing. I love you. I wonder what changed Rod. Congratulating herself for the preparations done on Friday, she gathered up the parts of a good dinner and set the table. The early summer evening, with the sea doing its magic, created a pleasant atmosphere.

When the men came in, Rodney surprised her by saying, "It's quite a nice place you have here, Mum."

"Yes, I think so. A bit small but enough. When the car is housed and dry, not coated by the salt winds, I'll be more pleased."

The evening passed pleasantly, as Rodney shared with them the more interesting side of his work. When he left them Howard and Mari, tired by a full day, decided that bed was an attractive destination. Howard pushed the two beds as close as was possible and they slept.

Chapter Six

"Hullo Winfred dear, how are you today?"

"Well, but how is the working mother now?"

"A bit tired still, but I could sleep later this morning. Win, I've got wonderful news for you. Yesterday flowed along so well, with very good communication. But, you'd never guess what happened. When I arrived home, Rodney was there helping Howard to build a carport to protect our car from the salt. Yes, he was pleasant to us. He stayed for dinner, which fortunately I had prepared on Friday. It was a lovely evening. It wasn't until today that Howard told me why he has recanted. It seems that very recently a certain lawyer in their firm has stolen money, embezzled a client's cash and it took some time before they found out the fact, so they're angry and ashamed that it happened."

"So now Rodney has learned how wicked the world is, and anyone can be caught out, including his own father."

"Exactly. It's not the way we'd like Rodney to learn, but he's now sympathetic towards us."

"As you say, this is another step in the journey to unity. I'd guess that Howard slept well last night. A man vindicated. But now, tell me, how was your afternoon yesterday?"

"Quite challenging, but I think I did okay. I told you I would have twin boys, which was walking into the dark for me. I felt it right to ask them how they wanted to put a lesson together. As I don't even know them, or how the twin factor would work, I had a good conversation with both. They are very intelligent and a delight. Obviously they have very good parents, so that's a blessing for me. I'm looking forward to having them play duets. That could be a great act."

"Hmm. That will be a novel way of playing the situation. I'm looking forward to that occasion."

"Yes, I hope that one day we'll make a presentation of what we're learning, to encourage the parents. I hope you'll come along to be an honorary grandmother. It's so encouraging for me to have your help for all this, Win. You are being like a mother. I do appreciate it, lots. And one Sunday, when I have the energy to wake up in the morning, I'll come to your church."

"Darling, we'd love to have you presence there. You'll be a joy in our worship."

"Jake, the angel with horny hands is coming this afternoon to help Howard with the car shelter. I have to check on things in the big house now. We expect a number of people may inspect it, today, tomorrow. The auction will actually be held in a big hall in town on Tuesday. I've got nervous tremors already. Yes, I know what to do about them, taught by you."

"Indeed, we are agreed that God is in control for a super-charged result."

"Good afternoon, ladies and gentlemen. As you know, we are here for the sale of number 18 Makepeace Heights. This beautiful house and garden package will be admired by the most discriminating buyers. Everything in it has been checked and found to be in impeccable condition. It is a house to please a family as well as certain features which will impress your guests. The main bedroom has Queen Anne style hand carved mahogany; the guest bedroom has unusual quality timber and features, the living rooms have comfort, charming décor and furniture. All the bathrooms are of high standard. As you will see by your document, the pieces of furniture will be sold as separate lots, room by room, after the sale of the house. Now, who will give me an opening bid? Yes Sir, thank you…"

Mari was sitting shivering in spite of the warm day. It was a surreal experience. This can't be happening; my house under the hammer, and the world looking into it. Here it is in black and white. It has to happen, but God is in control. I hope Howard will arrive soon … I can't understand what he's saying … five five six and five; five what, for heaven's sake? Gosh, how complicated, up by fives; now he's talking to one of the assistants. I gather there are some bidders out of sight in Auckland, bids coming by email. I suppose they came, looked, and went back to their business there, how can they manage? Six, six-five, seven, seven-two, seven-five, seven-eight, eight, up by twos, wow eight-six, more talk, nine, nine-two, nine-four, now they're discussing someone's ideas, Auckland again, nine-six, nine-eight, it's Auckland again, the same again, any more? Nine-nine wait; there we are, all done. A hammer banged.

"Thank you ladies and gentle men."

Mari was aware of a movement beside her. It was Howard. She could hardly hear his voice in the murmur of voices all round. "Was he saying what I think he said?"

Mari answered, "I don't know. I couldn't understand him."

The auctioneer was speaking again. "Ladies and gentlemen, we come to lot two, the mahogany bedroom furniture, six pieces hand carved; what am I bid? Six hundred, okay for a start but worth more; eight hundred, nine hundred…" His voice went on, hovering around sixteen to seventeen hundred, then seventeen fifty. "Where is Auckland? And seventeen-seven-five, any more? I am bid seventeen-seven-five, once, twice. Sold." The hammer sounded again. "Thank you sir."

"This is exhausting isn't it?" said Mari. "After this I need coffee and lunch."

"So do I. Here he is again."

"Ladies and gentlemen, lot three, guest bedroom suite, has appeal for the sensitive connoisseur, very unusual timber and design…"

"Or the more money than sense person," whispered Mari, stifling a giggle. But little competition finished by leaving a beaming buyer.

The next lot had more appeal for the new owner of the house, and fetched a good price, to Howard's satisfaction. Among the hubbub of voices Mari asked, "Can we go and buy lunch now?"

"Wait a bit. Our solicitor is here somewhere, keeping watch on our account, so we must talk to him now."

The following conversation was heart-warming and optimistic for long term results. Gerald Winchester was a middle-aged, experienced man who shook hands cordially, smiling. "I think we can be quite pleased. After the necessary costs are taken off, we can say, on the whole, a good sale."

Howard took Mari's hand while they scurried out the door. However, Winifred's caring expression slowed them as she reached out to Mari, hugging her. "Precious dears, are congratulations in order?"

Two smiling faces answered her.

"Yes, we think so," said Howard. "We're just going to have lunch. Would you like to have coffee with us?"

"Only if I'm not in the way. And, on condition that you let me come and help you with whatever work you have to do now, Mari. I expect you have pressing things to do at the house, and you have a very busy week."

"True, and I would love to have your company. Howard has to go back to work and I'll be having departure blues on my own."

"That's settled then," said Howard. "And thank you, Winifred, for being such a wonderful help to Mari, and for your moral support."

Indeed that week was packed with activities. Mari was longing for the moment of Sylvia's arrival, yet wishing for more time to fit things in. Mari was preparing for her Wednesday evening of teaching, and also cooking Howard's dinner.

"Are they actually arriving on Thursday evening?" she asked while peeling apples.

"The airlines say so. They'll be bribing the weather gods."

"Pooh, we have a much better God to trust in." She rolled up the pastry and dropped it over the pie dish. "Turn the oven off at the time I've written here. Enjoy it. I must get ready to leave."

"Have a good evening, sweetheart."

And she did, in spite of a few butterflies. She spoke as with equals to the teenagers, who apparently enjoyed her teaching. Thank you Lord, she whispered in her mind.

Friday morning arrived at last. Marilyn had been thinking anxiously during the night. Will Sylvia be shocked at the way we're living here? Perhaps she will have changed, being now a married woman and travelling the world with her husband. She might even despise me now. Thank goodness the sea was looking beautiful; sunlit waves rolling in with a mild breeze.

When the car arrived she rushed out to greet Sylvia. The warmth of the greeting was immediately calming. "My precious daughter! You look beautiful. Have you had a lovely trip?"

"Yes, it was terrific, but it's nice to be back. You look beautiful too, and happy. I didn't expect to see that. You look different. I was expecting you to be angry and … well, resentful, after what's happened to you and Daddy."

"I am different. What do you think of our little pied-a-terre?"

"It's nice," Sylvia answered carefully. "But the site, and the view! Ben will love this. You know how architects value a sea view."

"I have to say I'm enjoying living here, now we've worked like slaves to make it livable. Sand papering the walls and our fingers, painting and scraping the dirt. I've never worked so hard in my life."

"You must have felt heartbroken at leaving your lovely house, and coming to live in two rooms; so cramped."

"But it's cheap. We pay no rent, just enjoy it."

"And you're working again; teaching! That must have been hard for you to get into the job, and so quickly! How did you manage that, and why?"

"The why is simple, because Howard couldn't draw much money from the firm, it was in dire straits after Cobbles embezzled so much money. It was logical for me to teach, though the how wasn't easy. You see how this house isn't big enough, or really suitable for teaching. I prayed, my friend Winifred helping me, for a place to keep my piano. She found Mrs Wakelin, who was my onetime teacher, and asked her help. She was wonderful, inviting me to put the piano in her house, and what's more, handing a lot of her pupils to me. I've become a breadwinner, and enjoying it."

"Well, this is surely a tale of triumph over adversity. I'm almost speechless."

"Let's go into the house, while you absorb it then. We'll have coffee and muffins which I baked for you. You can tell me what you think of our home-grown paint job." Mari was watching Sylvia's face for signs of revulsion. But the smile was genuine and relaxed.

"You've done wonders, and I'm glad you've made muffins. I've been longing for some home made food all the time we've been travelling."

They settled into comfortable chairs and spoke of Sylvia's travels, in pleasant enjoyment.

"So where have you been and what did you see?" asked Mari.

"England, Spain, Italy and Israel. We've seen buildings, houses, churches and more. We've learned who planned, who built and when. We could write a book for architectural students. In fact I think Ben might do."

"So are you fed up with the subject?"

"Oh no, I'm still interested. I've absorbed a lot on the way. Yes, it has been a very interesting trip. But, Mum, I want to know more about how you achieved this metamorphosis, in such a short time. You're a different person, and survived such awful shocks. How did you do it?"

"Indeed it's been a shock. I thought I couldn't possibly live with it. But a few days after this terrible blow came to us, I happened to meet an old friend, Mrs Meldrum, my Sunday School teacher of long ago. I was only about twelve or thirteen at last sight of her. Then, that day, I went to the hardware shop to buy a few things, knowing I had no choice but to move in here. I met her, Winifred, in the shop. I was feeling ghastly, as you can imagine. I couldn't even teach piano to earn money. So when Winifred invited me to lunch at her house, I went and she encouraged me to tell the whole sad story. She kept telling me that I was her favourite pupil, which reminded me about that time. She was such a lovely person, who spoke beautifully about Jesus, how much He has done for us and how God loves us to an amazing degree. It was near that time when Daddy died, and I was ready to hear about Father God. I hoped He would comfort me, like another father, and He did so. After that I often prayed to Jesus, when things were difficult or sad and He helped me often. I loved Him." Marilyn was encouraged by Sylvia's rapt expression. "But, and I'm ashamed of this, I forgot to keep on praying. My life was so busy, with working for piano exams plus ballet and school exams; I knew that Mum and Daddy wanted me to do well. I simply forgot and when I met Howard we married and had babies, that was more so. We didn't even go to church. Our social life took off, that's probably the part you remember. We entertained sometimes, which seemed the right thing to do. My life was being pulled in different directions, music and so on. You know that part."

"Yes, I do remember that you were often on the phone, and you were out in the evenings when we had a baby sitter, and there would be someone in the kitchen, cleaning in your absence."

"I'm not proud of that part of my life, and I can almost laugh at myself now, shaken out of such a shallow existence. Music, yes, but the presumed friends who have disappeared, were obviously not worth anything. I owe a lot to Winifred and Mrs Wakelin, and of course, the Lord because, as I've asked for His mercy, He has so blessed me. He is in my heart and my body, always helping my life to run smoothly." Mari looked at her daughter to guess how the words had gone across.

In the pause that followed Sylvia drew a deep breath. "Whew! That's a great leap into the spiritual world isn't it? I think I hear you saying that you had a need, you prayed to Father God, and He comforted you in your need. So now , you believe in Him. Is that what you're telling me? But I see the effect on you. It must be working in your life. You surely were in need of help."

"Yes, exactly. I still am in need. I am teaching again, and every day brings its difficulties and problems. Howard is drawing only a small salary from the firm. It's going on okay with a lot of care. He doesn't want to put any staff off." Mari herself took a deep breath. "What a lot of talk. Let's have a rest from it. Would you like more coffee, another muffin? No? What about a walk along the beach? Would you need a jacket?"

"Yes, let's do that. I don't need a jacket."

Mari picked up a small towel. "I like to walk on the sand barefoot. It might be too low class for you, but I've fallen so far down the social scale, I don't care what anyone thinks. I know it's not a perfect picture beach but if it were there'd be a hundred houses and a thousand people on the beach in summer."

"Agreed. I think it's charming. Walking on sand barefoot is relaxing, especially after all that travel." There were small out crops of rock in which were a few tiny pools, homes for miniature creatures.

"Danny loves these pools. He's enchanted by the occupants; would like to take them home but Gordon tells him they would rather be here. Danny would like to live with me; but perhaps in the summer. Oh look, see that little fish, two centimetres long, and another." They bent over the pools, two close friends. Their shared delight was healing for the sadness Mari felt.

"I agree with Danny. These creatures are fascinating. I like to touch the little anemones and watch them close. That's being mean I know. I love watching the nature films on TV."

"I do too. Since I've been talking to God, I find myself praising Him for the wonderful world He's put us into. Now, I'm sorry, I want to avoid embarrassing you with talk about God. I'm aware that in the world there is so much loose talk, making fun of Christians. Sometimes its asked for, because someone is overdoing it in the presence of folk not inclined to think about the spiritual world. So I don't want to embarrass you and have you think I'm a loony. I am careful when I'm with Howard."

"No I don't think that, because I know you. You have too much good sense than to go overboard. I admire the way you're coping."

"I have to ask you to forgive me for not telling you about Jesus and His love for us. I ought to have read some Bible stories to you."

"But you did! I loved the story about the little lamb that was lost. The shepherd went out in the dark to find it, then He carried it back to its mummy. I think I did recognise some deeper spiritual things in your personality."

"Thank God I did that much. I've confessed to God and asked for forgiveness."

"But Mum, you weren't sinning, were you? Who did you cheat?"

"I have to say I've learned to think differently now, God's way. I've confessed my ingratitude, that I forgot to pray. I had pride. I wasn't doing terrible sins as the world sees them, like profanities, malicious gossip that hurt anyone, telling lies or dirty jokes, but I allowed it to go on in my presence. I was pretending to be friends with people who thought it was smart to cheat in business and evade taxes. Be clever, don't get found out." They paused briefly, in thought.

"This is all a grim tropic, isn't it? How did this get impressed on you?"

"Years ago, by Mrs Meldrum's teaching. And recently, I'm reading books that she loaned to me. I know now that God sees our hearts."

"Perhaps I ought to read these books. Recently we heard about builders who took the government money, did shoddy work and got rich while the buildings were falling down. It does go on."

"And brings poverty to the innocent on the way. What a ghastly topic. Let's go home quickly and find lunch. I made a bacon and egg pie because I know it's your favourite."

They turned and walked back home, waving a greeting to the very few people they saw on the way. While passing Jake's house, Mari waved to Nellie who was obviously busy in her garden. "Lovely people," said Mari, and told Sylvia how they had helped them from the first day.

The bacon pie was delicious to their sharpened appetites, when heated in the microwave.

"This feels like we're on holiday here," said Sylvia. "I could envy you. I don't know about winter but it's perfect now."

"True, the winter could be rough and windy. We'll have to plan heating, and how to insulate or something like that. The old chip heater idea could work, with off-cuts from builders. Another idea I'd like to work on is how to fit in a little bed for Danny, because he'd love to spend a night here occasionally."

They indulged in close mother-daughter talk for a little until Sylvia said, "I've an idea for a present for you, Mum. And don't say no, because you will really appreciate it." Mari looked at her with raised eyebrows. "Yes, absolutely. I want to take you shopping, a plumbing shop. You will choose a new toilet, and wash basin and shower to replace those well-used objects in there." She waved her hand at the bathroom, while smiling widely.

Mari's mouth dropped open, then she laughed. They both laughed, until Mari dropped into a chair. "I've heard of travel broadening your mind, but that makes me wonder what sort of things you've been doing. It was my birthday recently but what a present!"

"It's being married to an architect that makes the banal things seem very important. And I'm going to pay in advance for a plumber to install them. You'll choose what day he will come."

Marilyn sighed with pleasure. "Darling, it's more than generous of you. I did hate cleaning those things, because they never looked clean. You are a sweetheart."

"Let's go shopping," said Sylvia. "We have husbands to feed."

But Mari said, "I want to go to the bookshop first. I have arranged for you to meet a special friend of mine there."

Half an hour later, at the bookshop, they met up with Winifred who, in a very cordial introduction, said, "Like mother, like daughter! Sylvia, I'm delighted to meet you."

"It's mutual," said Sylvia. "I'm so impressed by the way my mother is cheerfully coping with all the difficulties in her life. I want to know how, and what books she's reading!"

"That's easy to answer. Mari and I have spent time with the Bible. I would recommend this one," she said, picking up a large book with *The Amplified Version of the Bible* written across its cover.

Mari was browsing some text books.

Win continued, "Mari dear, I can tell you one of the best teachers of how to live the Christian life is James, in the New Testament. The Book of James is not boring but challenging, and all Christians ought to read it often."

Her face lit up. "Thank you, Win."

After Sylvia purchased the Bible, Mari said, "Well, we had better find some food for our husbands."

"Bless you, my darlings. See you tomorrow," said Win as the women hurried out the door.

As day follows night, Saturday was as busy and fulfilling as Mari expected it to be. When relaxing at home later, she phoned Sylvia and Ben to invite them to visit on Sunday.

"Yes, but not till after lunch. You will not want an early start, likewise Ben. He wants to catch up with some friends as well."

They arrived on a pleasant day, as every one hoped for Ben's first visit. He stepped out of the car, entranced, and said, smiling, "You people are clever to buy such a neat site for a house, the cliff behind and miles of view in front, all-day sun. I've got just the right plan for a house here just behind this wooden thing. What size section, where's your back boundary?"

"Sorry Ben," said Howard. "I've never got round to finding our boundaries. This is what you'd call emergency housing."

"But it's got terrific potential. It would be a sin not to build here; something low, big panes of glass soaking up the sun. There are all sorts of sun-absorbing materials and ways of storing heat and electricity. Trees already there as a back-drop!" He waved his arms enthusiastically.

"I told you so!" said Sylvia.

"I'll have to hire a surveyor. Or look at a town plan, if it exists."

They sat down and talked for half an hour, then another car arrived. "It's Gordon and Tracy and the children," Mari cried. "What am I going to feed everyone with?"

But Tracy, as she emerged from the car, said, "Don't panic, I've brought our tea. It's enough for everyone."

There was much laughter and talk and cuddling of the children.

Danny ran off to the beach with his bucket, while the others simply enjoyed the company. Mari spoke little. She was almost crying with happiness, her heart singing thank you Lord, while she sat in a big chair holding her sweet-smelling grand-daughter and her doll. The sun shone on the sea, blessing them all.

Mari had been longing to get her hands into the soil, to plant summer salad plants. Came a Tuesday which was fairly free, and she brought out their tools. It was fun to fork up the big weeds to find what they were hiding. The little fruit on the trees were swelling in a promising way. A few raspberry canes were found, their prickles demanding gloves. The soil was semi-sand and easy to fork.

I suppose I should have string and plant in rows, she told herself. But getting them started was urgent work and it doesn't really matter, she said hopefully. Unskilled but optimistic, she had bought lettuce, cucumber and tomato plants. I hope Howard can help me do the staking. It's beginner's luck for us both.

And although the rows were rather straggly she felt pleased with her first attempts.

Howard, arriving home in the late afternoon sun, found Mari trailing a fork through the soil.

"First time I've seen you in the garden. Do you know what you're doing?"

"No, I'm learning as I go along. Like you will be, I hope."

"Not sure about that. But you're a good mate." He dropped an arm around her shoulder and kissed her lightly. "If you come into work with me I'll give you a job."

"A job? What do you mean?"

"There's a bit of high pitched moaning lately."

"What? High pitched? You mean the women at work? What are they unhappy about?"

"The ladies' rest room I suppose. I don't know. We blokes aren't fussy about job conditions. We simply get on with the job. Some women might be threatening to leave."

"Oh. How am I supposed to help?"

"I guess, be a sympathetic ear. I haven't the time now. They've been doing well and I don't want a general exodus. Don't want to break a good ship."

"So when and how do I do this? Will I be on the payroll?"

"Well, maybe. We'll have to allocate money for expenses, to keep them happy. You're good at organising things."

Marilyn considered thoughtfully, running soil through her fingers. "It'll be hard for me to find the time now I have to be so many people. I'll have a go. Give me a few days to think. In the meantime I'll come in and dish the dinner. You can tell me I'm good at gardening."

The next day Mari phoned Winifred. "Howard wants me to be the H.R. officer. I'll have to talk to these women sometime. Dear Win, tell me how to manage this?"

"You will become their friend. Invite them for a cup of tea, or coffee. You can charm them, talk to them and ask what is troubling them."

"How, though without spending much money? If I take them out..." Her voice trailed away.

"Let me help you. Wouldn't you be able to use their morning tea room? Start by pinning up an invitation, to all ladies, day and time. I'll make two dozen muffins, two flavours. Freshly made; you bring the butter and some nice jam. We cut and butter while they watch. I bet they'll gobble them up. Let me be the waitress while you organise the conversation. You'll do it beautifully."

Thoughtfully Mari said, "You make it sound easy. But it's work for you. I ought to do it myself."

"You need help and I'd like to make it easy for you. They'll love you for it. Good for the firm. Happy workers, you know."

"You really are wonderful, Win, and Howard will be grateful."

"That's settled then. And ask Howard to come and eat a muffin with us. Let me know what day you decide."

The invitation was given, and the women responded with a gentle buzz. The senior woman, always somewhat severe in her black suit, was prepared to be gracious to the boss's wife. It had been, after all, a tricky few weeks for everybody.

Mari had dressed carefully in a smart suit and careful make up. Women notice everything. Winifred, always smiling, stood beside Mari and was introduced. With cups of tea and coffee, they sat around the table and sampled the still warm fragrant cakes with little murmurs of appreciation.

"I'm so glad to meet you all," said Mari. "You are the glue that holds this firm together. We all know that the men need lots of support, the poor dears, so I'd like to know how you feel about working here. Be candid, be honest, and tell me about anything that upsets or irritates you. Would you like to start, Mrs Sturt?" addressing the senior lady who took a sip of her tea, then began to speak.

Following her, the conversation was easy. Mari suggested that they show her their personal rooms, and invited them to suggest changes or improvements.

Howard was summoned from his office, with the promise of a muffin, to take a look at the list of the ladies' requests. He read the list of items with sympathy, saying he would try to supply the smaller items as soon as possible, while putting more expensive work into the future, when their profits would be higher. "As I'm sure you understand, our finances have been badly compromised by certain events beyond my control."

Altogether it was a well-spent afternoon, they agreed. Mari and Winifred washed the cups as Howard praised them for a good result.

"Thank you sir," said Mari. "When shall I get the raise?"

She opted to go with Win, detouring to practise on her piano. "What would I do without you as a friend?" she queried.

"Just as well as you are doing. I'm pleased to help. Good for my self-esteem too. Bless you."

Enjoying the summer evening while looking at the growing garden and watering the little green plants was a satisfying end to the day. The feeling of well-being overflowed.

I feel I could create something else now. What shall I do for a bed for Danny? She sat and stared at Howard's desk. It's big. Over or under it? She rolled on the floor as a child might. The drawers take space, but the rest of the floor area might be enough, with feet out of the end. A sleeping bag on a lilo, a pillow, and with a big rug laid over to enclose the tiny room. Yes, I'll try him under there. He might even like it!

Soon after Howard left for work, the phone rang. "Hullo Mum, it's Sylvia. Sorry to ring you early, but I've just realised I need to pick up my stuff from the big house. I'm still able to, I hope. Would you come with me?"

"Of course, if you come and pick me up. Come soon. We'll be able to have lunch together." The phone rang again, almost immediately. It was Winifred. "I've been promising myself to have you and Sylvia to lunch with me, together or one at a time, if you'd rather."

"You are clever, because we've just arranged to be in town today. Thank you, we'd love to."

"Bless you darlings. I've been looking forward to this."

The visit to the big house was bitter-sweet for Mari and Sylvia, each knowing that her future would be different. Their happy memories had passed for ever, while the future could only be guessed at. Sylvia's future depended so much on her husband's wishes.

For Mari, she was depending on the Lord, a belief which occasionally let her down, as she thought how much easier life would be if Cobbles had not stolen their money. But, she told herself sternly, many things had worked out perfectly in recent weeks; proof to her that someone was organising her daily blessings, and she actually felt happy at times. That Someone must be her Lord who strengthened her internally, with a song in her heart. Often, in fact, she felt that she might bubble over in happiness. I have to suppress that, or someone will report me as being barmy.

And so they worked together, mother and daughter, laughing at silly little memories while forcing back tears. They discussed which pieces of furniture must go into storage, or go to a temporary home with Tracy. Leaving the garden was terribly sad for Mari so she softened it a little by digging up a few small plants and taking cuttings. Thankful for Sylvia's company, she eventually decided they must go to Winifred's for lunch.

Their arrival was just as pleasant as Mari expected. Win hugged them both, exclaiming again at their similarity. Mari protested that her daughter was by far the more beautiful; "I'm a wrinkled old hag by comparison," she said.

"You're not a wrinkled hag, and I remember you as a girl when you were beautiful and very like Sylvia is now. You have good bones and lovely eyes. As a person you're beautiful and under the skin you are also."

"Winifred's right, Mum. I know when I was small I used to think how very pretty you were. I hoped to grow up like you. Just ask Daddy what he thinks and remembers."

"Absolutely, and I should add that the personality shines through also. Let's go and have lunch. Now, serve yourselves, have chutney on your meat and mayonnaise with salad."

They chattered on about Sylvia's travels and her aims for work. "She can teach piano if she wants to. She's sufficiently qualified. Would you like us to set up together, darling?"

"Maybe. At this moment I'm interested in what Mum's been learning from you recently, Mrs Meldrum. It's something substantial, considering all that's happened."

"There, I said that you are very alike, searching for important truth. But I didn't invite you here to load you with a sermon. And please call me Win."

"Well, I can't help being amazed by Mum's acceptance of the situation, horrible as it was, and how well organised she is now, in only a few weeks. The house and the mortgage have gone, they live simply in a tiny but pleasant beach house. And the piano lessons are going like clockwork, with some money coming in. I expected to arrive home to a terrible shambles, plus anger and bitterness. How has this come about, so soon?"

Win was thoughtful. "If we go back some years, we see that Mari was living as a Christian, aware of Jesus playing a large part in her life, even though, as she told me, she almost forgot to think about and to pray to Him. But God, in his mercy, has kept His hand upon her. He knows the future. He showed Mari that beach cottage a year or so earlier, when Howard had the money to buy it. So when the crash came they had that as a refuge. You've heard how it was a lot of work to clean it up and repair it to make it livable. God, I believe, sent Jake the builder to help, with his skills. All these factors were in place years previously. We can say that God was watching Mari and teaching her faith even when she wasn't truly conscious of Him. She would be ready for that future."

"Then, super coincidence, Win and I met in the hardware shop, when I was almost collapsing at the shock of it all. From that day, with God's help, and a lot of Win's, I was able to make some sort of progress."

"Coincidences don't exist with God. He had that planned, of course, with Mrs Wakelin waiting in the wings to answer Mari's prayer for a home and a place for her piano lessons. Sylvia, your

Mum has certainly got recovery power and grit in large quantities, to get straight into teaching, after a lapse of how many years?"

"I do agree, and being mobile on a bicycle; the rich Mrs Alton shopping with a bike! No one would see that without jaw-dropping. I'm proud of you, Mum."

"She's right, Mari. That proves to me that my early estimate of your personality was absolutely right. It's a privilege to help you. You're not like some I know."

"I know I'm blessed in having this family. I haven't told you Win, that this girl has bought me a beautiful birthday present. A new toilet, shower and washbasin. I can hardly wait until it's installed."

"And in the meantime ... we'd better hurry that tradesman!"

They all laughed until their sides ached.

Winifred invited them to find some more comfortable chairs, "so we can enjoy looking at the garden as we talk."

"Sylvia dear, I'd love to hear more from you, about your travels. Your impressions of Israel for one, and I think Win would also."

"I'll try, though the things I recall may not be of interest to you. Ben has lived there with his father and mother for some years, after they moved from Italy. Perhaps they are not truly immersed in the Israeli life-style as much as others are. Did they go to the synagogue, you're asking me. I think Ben may have gone with his father once, but without me. I think it's a very masculine culture. So the Shabbat, as they call Saturday, is definitely a no work day. It's strangely quiet from sunset Friday to sunset Saturday. No busses or trams, people walk. In the hotels you have to get your own breakfast and lunch; the food is left out from Friday night, same thing with lights. Shops are shut, until Saturday sunset. Then, they all come to life, with music and dancing in the streets. They seem very happy and lively people, and interesting. Food too, so many different things to try." Sylvia sipped from her glass of water.

"If you could forgive another question, darling," said Mari, "I'm very interested in Israel because it's the historical birth place of Jesus. He is important to me and Win. Were any places pointed out to you?"

"Um, in a vague way I was aware of some tourist busses. Some did a trip to Samaria and places out in the desert. It's terribly dry and lifeless because it doesn't rain often. They have very deep wells, and water is rationed carefully. We saw the lake of Galilee. Ben took me to the Dead sea, that's interesting and useful. They extract minerals from it, a source of income."

"What else did Ben show you, Sylvia? Buildings?"asked Win.

"Oh yes. Lot's of new ones of unusual shapes, the architects are very clever as you'd expect. And some very old ones of quarried stone, each fitted to the next stone, no cement. We saw the old wall of Jerusalem more than once. That's amazing, to think of it's age. There were some Jewish men who looked very solemn and strange, walking in the streets and standing near the very old wall. They had black beards, black suits and big black hats. Someone told me that they are Rabbis. They take their religion very seriously. All the other people were normal and bright looking, doing their shopping in very smart shops. I didn't see any beggars or down and outs. Signs and titles were in Hebrew. We heard a lot of other languages as well as English, especially tourists."

"That's actually why I asked about buildings, Sylvia. Some of my Christian friends have been to Israel to look at the famous historical sites, where Jesus was associated and active. But of course, if your husband is Jewish he would not have been interested."

"I guess not. But I'm puzzled, what is it in this Israel? Mum has told me why Jesus is important to her, yet now I think I would not dare ask Ben or anyone. In the hotel, when I was waiting for Ben, I heard English tourists talking about tripping about to look at places where He was supposed to have been. They thought it was great!"

"This is my fault. I didn't educate you, as Win did for me at Sunday school. I'm ashamed that I let you grow up in ignorance." said her mother. "I didn't even give you a Bible."

"We'll soon remedy that," said Win. "I have several. I'll lend you the easiest to read one, and I'm not insulting you. It will give you the modern English translation. Let me go fetch some. Back in a minute." In fact, it was thirty seconds when she returned, hands full of books. "Have a look at these. They all have qualities to recommend them. Occasionally it's helpful to compare two translations for the shades of meaning. That doesn't mean that some Bibles are wrong, just historically early or later in the translating."

"But can't we get confused as to the truth, if they're different?" asked Mari.

"No, the truth is very carefully checked by scholars before it's printed. Somewhere in the Bible it says that 'all scripture is good for edification'. That is the amazing thing about the Bible, we know it is 'the living word'. The words can speak to many people in surprising ways, and the Lord gives our minds an assurance that He is indeed telling us."

"That sounds wonderful," said Sylvia. "I think it's time for us to go to the right bookshop and buy our own books, don't you think, Mum?"

"Definitely," said Mari, scribbling names on a list. "I've been meaning to do that, but my life is so busy. This way we can choose and swap as we feel."

"No time like the present. My car is at your disposal, Mum. Thank you for lunch, Winifred."

"Indeed, thank you for feeding us in all ways, Win dear."

"Bless you, my dears. Come again soon."

"You know, this bookshop is the perfect place for us, especially me. Danny's birthday is very close. I'd like to buy him books about animals, especially sea creatures. You know how he is fascinated by them. I want good coloured pictures, some words which people will read and then he'll learn to read the names."

"Excellent idea," said Sylvia. "I wonder who'll enjoy it most, Grandma or Danny?"

"It runs in the family. I adore the selection they have here. I'd like to live in a bookshop."

With difficulty they made their choices, and tore themselves away from the shop. Next were food items, something quick and easy to "feed their animals", as Sylvia put it. At home, Mari reluctantly put her books down and set about cooking dinner. Howard would bring the car home for her. It was her evening to teach, and so she disciplined her thoughts. When I get home I can go to bed and read.

Howard was working at his desk when she did return home, and thankfully made a milk drink, served him and took her books to bed. It was pure bliss, until she fell asleep. Howard picked up the book from her sleepy hand and began to read, highly interested in the story titled *The Rough Road, How to Survive It.*

Two days later, Tracy rang Marilyn. "How's life?'

"Just coping. In between looking after Howard and doing music, I rush out to the garden and plant something new, and gloat over the green growing things, and tell myself that I'm clever, now I'm a real gardener."

"I have two reasons for asking. I'm really interested, and because it's Danny's birthday very soon."

"Yes, I know that. Am I invited?"

"Of course you are, in various ways. One reason is that he wants to celebrate part of the day at your place.'

Mari gave a gulp before answering. "Oh, I am flattered!"

"Don't worry, it won't be difficult at all for you because you'll be away working that Saturday. Gordon and I will watch over the little darlings so that they don't drown, or run over your precious veggie garden. Your Grandson thinks you're a marvellous person in many ways, one being that you own the beach!"

Mari laughed. "It sounds as though I'm going up in the world again! Bless him, tell him that he's welcome, with his friends. I'm pleased to say that we have sparkling new bathroom furniture now for their use."

"That's lovely, thank you Mari. And, we're bringing them back to our place for the party tea. There'll be no sticky crumbs left at your house, only at mine, worse luck."

On Sunday afternoon, Mari rang Tracy. "How did it go Tracy? I'm all ears."

"A real success, fine weather, happy kids, especially the beach part. You are a renowned grandma, because you own that stretch of beach."

"That's what happens when you buy a piece of land at the end of a gravel road. May they never seal it."

"Well, Danny was in his element as co-owner of it, telling them what to look for, then saying 'This is my special part of it, these are my very own baby fish. We can feed them some bread and they'll get to know me.' The delightful thing is that they're young enough to believe him; for the time being. That set of rocks at your end of the beach is a wonderful gift. You should have seen them, four little boys crouching around that pool. Gordon took photos of them. We'll show you."

"I'm so glad it's a hit with them. I believe it is a gift of God; among others."

"And thank you for the books; Danny loves them, so do we. It makes a parents' job easier."

On Wednesday morning, a fine early summer day with a light breeze and nesting blackbirds singing in the trees, Mari was planning to do the minimum of housework plus food preparation for her evening of piano teaching. I hope I can spend a little time in the garden. The phone rang. It's very early for someone to ring. I hope it's not urgent.

But it was Tracy, and she sounded anxious. "Are you very busy, Mari? I'm worried about Danny. He's obviously unwell. I think he's feverish and doesn't want his breakfast. This is so unlike our strong, bold Danny."

"Have you rung a doctor?"

"Yes, and the nurse told me to bring him in. The doctor will see him as soon as possible."

"So you'd like my help, to be with you and look after Melissa?"

"Exactly that, if you are able. I'm sorry to rush at you."

"Understood. Can you come and pick me up? Sorry I haven't the car today."

"Of course. Is fifteen minutes okay?"

"See you then." Mari rushed to change into decent clothes, ready for who knew what might happen. She thought to ring Howard to warn him that she might need the car.

A short time later, Mari sat in the doctor's waiting room cuddling Melissa and reading a picture book to her. "Mummy will be back in a couple of minutes. Look, darling, a pussy cat. Pussy says miaow."

Melissa pointed to the bright pictures while Mari's mind was whirling with the memory of recent happy days. How suddenly grief could strike. Strong little Danny, now four years old, and seeming invincible just the day before.

An office attendant came to speak to her. "Mrs Alton? Mr Alton has just left a message for you. Your car will be delivered here for you in about half an hour."

"Thank you." Mari tried to smile gratefully. She continued to talk and read to Melissa, while ignoring the other people waiting. I can't bear to think of the troubles that they might have.

Very soon the doctor's nurse came to speak to her. "Mrs Alton, your daughter-in-law would like you to come in and talk, if you please. Let me help you with your things."

Mari followed her into a single room where Tracy held a very ill-looking Danny.

The doctor introduced himself, saying, "Mrs Alton, as you are no doubt aware Danny is seriously ill. I want to get him admitted to hospital immediately. I could order an ambulance; I don't know how many minutes that would take. Perhaps you, Grandma and Mother would prefer to take him yourselves now? Could you manage? He's quite heavy."

Tracy and Mari spoke together. "Yes, we can do it now." They wrapped a blanket round Danny.

"I'll ring ahead to the hospital so that an orderly with a trolley will meet you at the car. Now, suppose I carry Danny to your car myself. You are close?"

"Yes, that will be very helpful, thank you," said Tracy.

They made a small procession to the car nearby; the doctor with Danny, Mari carrying Melissa, Tracy with the admission letter.

When Danny was settled on the back seat, Mari told Tracy that she would wait there, for the short time for her car to be delivered. "I'll keep Melissa with me to leave you free, then I'll catch up with you at the hospital."

Entering the hospital at the emergency entrance, Mari was directed to the casualty department. Danny, unnaturally still and unresponsive lay on a bed while Tracy sat close holding his hand. She looked up, smiling her gratitude to Mari. "The doctor here thinks he may have meningitis. He has vomited a little; his head and neck are sore. They are going to start antibiotic treatment immediately. He'll be admitted to the children's ward."

Mari nodded her understanding. "You've started treating him early," she said. "I'm praying for him, and now Winifred and a couple of her friends are also. We know the Lord likes to heal little children."

"Thank you," said Tracy. A few tears rolled down her cheeks. "I want to stay with him for a few hours, anyway."

"Well, I have the afternoon ahead of me, and teaching this evening. Suppose that I keep Melissa for the moment, and she might like to have a sleep at my place. Then, later, I can shop for some easy dinner for you and me and our husbands. I'll have to pick up Howard later, and we can bring Gordon into the picture. Does Gordon know?"

"Not completely. It's near lunch time. I'll ring soon." Mari was afraid that as Melissa tired, she would become upset at being separated from her mother, and so she planned to give Melissa lunch and a sleep quite soon. Grabbing some toys, she took the little girl to the beach house, had a tiny walk on the beach and cooked eggs for lunch. That went well so Mari found a book to read to her, and lay down beside her on the bed. Melissa was pleased to co-operate and fell asleep quickly. That gave Mari time to prepare meals for both families and to groom herself. Pupils can notice details of dress.

Gordon and Tracy returned home in the early evening and Mari dropped off Melissa. Tracy was tired and tense, having been told to return home for the night. "Danny has a special nurse at night and you must get your sleep. He's doing okay." They made plans for the morning.

Morning felt as though a black cloud covered the sky, even though the early summer day was as brilliant as usual. After breakfast Tracy took Melissa to Mari, knowing she would be perfectly cared for by her Grandma, with books and toys. She certainly looked happy, walking with Mari on the beach.

Tracy entered the children's ward and Danny's single room. Donning an isolation gown she approached his bed, and was disturbed that he didn't notice her. He was breathing very quietly, eyes closed and flushed, but immobile.

"Danny?" she spoke softly, then sought out a nurse for information. "Tell me, is Danny going to be all right?"

"I'll find his nurse. She'll tell you. Here she is."

Nurse Greve looked very kind. "You're Danny's Mum? Yes, we're watching closely, giving fluids, sponging him, antibiotics and frequent temperature checks. He's very sleepy but he does wake when we give fluids. Would you like to sit with him, giving drinks at half hourly intervals? He'll probably recognise you. You will be good for him, and we shall oversee his progress. I'll show you the chart on which to record how much he drinks."

Tracy was cheered that she said "progress" and was pleased to be able to help. When the doctor looked in to check, she was further pleased, believing that she was part of the team. He spoke calmly and quietly to her, raising her spirits.

Gordon arrived at the high school feeling despondent and somewhat irritated by the chatter, shouts and general cacophony which is normal at the start of a school day. He said his usual "Good morning" to his colleague who taught physics in the next room, Paul Chang. He was now known as Mr Chang, though previously on his arrival from China his name was Li Chang.

"Are you all right, Gordon?" asked Paul, with his usual smile, some concern on his face.

"Yes thank you Paul. I'm just worried about my son Danny. He had to go into hospital yesterday. He's very ill."

"Ooh, I am so sorry. He is ill, you say. What is it?" In his careful, slightly accented voice, there was no doubt about his deep concern.

"The doctors say he's probably got meningitis. My wife's in the hospital now helping to look after him. She's taken our little girl to her grandma for the day."

"That is serious I know. We can pray that he will recover quickly."

"Thank you," murmured Gordon, in some surprise, walking to his desk. What a strange thing to say, he thought. He picked up chalk to prepare the first math lesson on the black board. What am I doing, he asked himself. What did we work on last? Where's that text book gone to? The kids will be here in ten minutes. What did Paul say? He forced his brain to concentrate on math.

As the morning slowly passed, Tracy felt very alone in spite of a nurse in and out of the room. She longed for some sympathetic discussion, to share her worry. Danny was at least drinking fluids as she lifted his head but he slipped back into whatever state of consciousness prevailed.

I wish Mari could come, or who was that friend that used to pray? Oh God, help me to pray. Please will you heal our precious Danny. The ward noises, voices and an occasional cry drew her attention. So many sick children. Please look after them God.

Then, a voice softly called her name, "Tracy." She looked up to see Winifred standing in the doorway.

"Yes, please come in." With relief, Tracy stood to welcome Win. They talked in whispers. "I'm so glad you came, Winifred. I've been trying to think how to pray to God to heal Danny."

They hugged and returned to his bedside. Tracy showed her how Danny would swallow his fluids, before lapsing into sleep. "He is all right, isn't he, Win? I'm afraid he's unconscious."

"The Lord has Danny in his hand, and that sleep is healing. We can say thank you to the Lord. We keep on praising and thanking God for this healing, in Jesus' Name. Agreed?"

"Yes, I agree. Thank you, Lord Jesus."

In mid-afternoon Gordon found himself with a free period, as happened occasionally. Usually he was pleased to catch up on marking exercise books but today his thoughts were with his son Danny, and Tracy who was looking after him. He leaned his elbows on the desk, supporting his aching head. Suddenly he was aware that someone was standing in the doorway.

Paul's gentle voice said, "Excuse me, Gordon. Can I interrupt you?"

Gordon was not pleased, but realised he could have closed the door earlier. "It's all right, Paul. Come in." He motioned towards a chair.

"I sympathise with you. My family also has had severe illness. We lived in China under Communist rule. It is very restrictive, we are not allowed to worship God, to read the Bible. We love God. He is kind and loving, and so are we. But Communism says there is no God. We are not allowed to talk about the Bible or sing hymns. Then people report us, they tell lies, and get a reward."

Gordon was feeling impatient with this narrative, but obviously here was a man who had experienced suffering. He had to listen.

Paul's gentle voice continued. "Because my brother was put in prison for speaking about the Bible, Communist leaders in our town were very angry. His little boy was very sick, I think it was meningitis, but the leaders say there would be no medicine for this sick child. We go to the house at night, sit in the dark, and pray quietly that Jesus heal Li Chen, my nephew. We have faith in Jesus, and He gives us peace in our hearts. Next day, he is healing, almost well. We thank God and praise Him, quietly. We have joy in our hearts. That is why we love God and worship Him, because we have this joy, all the time. Communists have no joy. They quarrel, they lie and cheat and pay people for lying. Some, at the top, lie and cheat so they get rich, live in luxury. But the many, many poor work hard for little money. They have no joy."

Gordon had been watching Paul's face with interest. So here is an educated man, highly talented he knew, apparently believing in God and willing to say it out loud! His anxiety for Danny gave him some cause to question Paul. He glanced at his watch, and said, "Shall we go to the staff room for coffee?"

"Yes indeed, we have a little time."

While walking there Gordon said, "I'm sorry to sound disbelieving. But how do you know God exists? Or if He does, that He would want to help me or Danny?"

"You are right to ask. I know in my mind that He exists, I feel the joy, I see answers to prayers that we have made to Him. I read the Bible which tells me about God's love for me, for us." They took their coffee to a table and sat. "With my family and Christian friends we tell one another how Jesus helps us. We have so many signs of God helping us, even more in these times when the Communists make our life so difficult; that is their speciality. We have no freedom. We are told what to do, what to say. We dare not speak against Communism. It is terribly difficult to leave, unless someone helps you. My father prayed to God and we got away with very little money, so in New Zealand we are poor but we can find work. Then my brother and I went to university. My father was happy, because we were not allowed to study in China. We were sad at leaving our family but we can work here and send money to our families." Paul drained his cup of coffee, and glanced at his watch.

"Yes, time to move, but thank you for telling me. I can see you've had a hard life, and you are still helping to support your family. That's amazing," Gordon said, thinking of his own household bills and his mortgage. They walked back to their classrooms.

"But you will not mind if I ask God to heal your little boy?"

"No, that is kind of you. Thank you." They parted as boys erupted into the corridors. Gordon had felt drawn to Paul, almost as to a somewhat older brother.

Chapter Seven

Tracy found she felt more relaxed after Win arrived. They spoke in whispers and prayed easily, to Tracy's surprise. It felt the normal thing to do, in Win's company. Both women felt united in speaking to God as the child lay sleeping. Jesus loves him so much, Tracy realised, as she and Win were in such perfect agreement of thoughts and words. This is an atmosphere of love. I feel as though I've come home, and I want to stay in this atmosphere. I don't understand why I've never felt like this before, but I'm home now.

Win stood, saying, "I have to leave you now, but I'll keep praying. Would you like to come out for a few minutes, just to have some fresh air and refresh your mind?"

They moved gently, glancing back to check on the sleeping child. Encountering a nurse, Tracy said, "I'll be back in a few minutes."

She nodded, smiling calmly.

After five minutes of enjoying the gentle summer air Tracy returned and decided to give another drink to Danny. Lifting his head as usual, she saw a flicker of his eyelids, and he gazed at her face for about half a minute.

"Danny," she said softly, her heart thumping with joy, hoping that he would speak. But he slept again, while she whispered, "Thank you Lord."

As soon as the time neared school closing she left the room and went outside to ring Gordon. Her own voice excited, she told him, "I think Danny woke and recognised me." It may have been a little exaggeration, but it was worth it to hear his voice brighten. She shared this scrap of news with Winifred and Mari, and the phone lines rang with singing praise.

Tracy returned home in the evening, convinced that Danny was improving, and telling Gordon about how she and Winifred had spent time together praying for his healing. In return, Gordon told her about Paul Chang who had also prayed for Danny.

She said, "That's wonderful! I'm excited about the fact that you have a Christian helping us by praying."

Tracy put Melissa to bed then, feeling the stress of the day, fell into bed herself and slept happily. But Gordon stayed awake for some time, relishing his new friendship. A man to admire, who had survived severe trials but who looked happy and confident in his adopted country.

The following day Gordon and Paul met in the staff room at lunch time.

Gordon couldn't help smiling, so Paul asked, "Is it good news?"

"I think, yes. A little sign, Tracy tells me. But I'd like to talk to you, somewhere more private. Your room or mine?"

"Yes. A good idea. Your room, let's go. Ah, the Lord hears our prayers. So often He has helped me through dangerous moments."

"Thank you for praying for Danny's healing." They walked together, comfortable friends. "Would you like, sometime, to tell me about your dangerous moments?"

"I am pleased to do that. Is today a suitable time?"

"Yes, if you have time to spare? Sorry, these chairs are so hard. I have been thinking about your life, how you could be angry about the way you were treated. Tell me, how did you live; were your lives in danger?"

"Yes, often. People in our town knew if we were Christian. We lived quietly but they watched, they suspected often and watched to see when to report our meetings, because they got paid. At night, I would hear footsteps walk along past our house. They would hesitate, probably looking at the windows. I think, will someone knock hard on our door? I would sit silent, praying, Lord, make them walk away. I would wait. When they were gone, I whispered, thank you Lord. That was why my brother was put in prison. He read Bible stories to his child in bed."

Gordon was shocked at the horrible implications.

Paul looked distressed. "But you know, in China life is cheap, a great deal of the time. When Mao and Communism came into power, they promised everything would be good. Hungry peasants said, Yes we want communism, but those in power made crazy mistakes, it was worse than before. Mao took peasants to make steel, so they couldn't grow food. There was starvation everywhere, millions died. Many times stupid laws are passed and the poor die. Commune officials took grain from the peasants and they died of starvation. Mao said, 'A good woman can make a meal with nothing.' Only the officials have access to food markets. Extortion is practised frequently, on anyone who has worked hard to make a living. Then Mao invented the cultural revolution, and untrained academics were sent out to till the land. There was more and more mismanagement, wasted brains as well as food. Many of our relatives died. I don't know how we survived."

Gordon shook his head sympathetically. "I see why your father wanted a better life for you. How did your father leave to come to New Zealand?' asked Gordon. "Was he rich?"

"No, but our heavenly Father is rich. My father worked for some high-up men, they liked him. My father is very clever with his hands. One said, 'I can pay you well.' He said, 'I want to leave China. Please help me and my family.' Then my father and mother

95

prayed for many days to God. Then, a message came, be ready to leave on a certain day. It will be a long voyage to Australia and New Zealand. Pick up money from me, tell no one."

"So these were your mother and father, you and your brother, his wife and your nephew? He's a young child."

"Very young. The captain of the ship told us to disembark in Auckland. But we had very little money, hardly enough to buy food, no money for a hotel. We prayed, we thought perhaps Christians would help. We went to a church, not a very big one but we prayed and found the minister. He was very kind. We told him we had come from Communist China. Then he took us to a church elder, to his house. His wife was a very kind lady, she gave us food and cups of tea. This elder was also very kind. He said, 'We will find you somewhere to live.' He says, 'You are refugees, you have no entry pass, but the New Zealand government will help you perhaps.'"

"And were you able to speak well to them in English, to tell your story?"

"My father had learnt English for many years, because he was hoping to leave China. It was very difficult for us to learn, but my father studied late at night, secretly you know, and prayed every day, asking God to help us to leave China. My brother and I tried to learn too. How else can we live outside China?"

"You all have courage," said Gordon. "I admire you. You must have worked very hard."

"Yes, God helped us. The church minister found us sponsors. They talked to city councillors, found us a house that we could share, helped us to find jobs and pay rent for the house. We all worked, dull and hard jobs, my mother and sister-in-law too. But we were safe, no more threat of prison. We were so happy when we all went to church, sang hymns, prayed out loud. The good people at church became our friends. They gave us some clothes too and bicycles. We were very grateful so we tried to help them, worked for them."

"You deserved help. But tell me, did you get your education easily? You have been to university in New Zealand?"

"The education people were very kind to me. They offered me free education. I wanted to go to uni, and they told me to go to high school, one or two years, and do the university entrance exams. I liked math and physics, and got good marks. This is in Auckland where we were living, and the uni offered me a place. I had a night job too, so I could become a teacher."

"Good grief, man, you put me to shame. Don't tell me you still have a night job?"

"No, at least not often," said Paul modestly, dropping his eyes.

Gordon studied the smooth, young-looking cream skin of his friend. "It's a privilege for me to know you. Will you apply for citizenship?"

"Yes, we have done so. It's a privilege to be living here." Paul laughed at Gordon, mimicking his words.

"Your story is amazing. Has God really answered your prayers and saved your lives as you say, in spite of that intense regime, so powerful, so heartless?"

"I believe so, yes. My father and I, for many years we have believed the Bible and that God says He loves us, to bring us to eternal life. We believe, we trust him. I hear His voice in my mind, I talk to Him and He comforts me, often. I look at the beautiful world He has made for us to live in and I think, He is beautiful. I believe He is the creator. I have a deep relationship with Him, and a lot of joy. You know, relationships are what give meaning to our lives." There was a pause.

Gordon was thoughtful, thinking of his wife and children. Indeed, that's the nitty-gritty. "I have to believe what you say, because you and your friends have many answers to your prayers, while the Communists are so harsh in their treatment."

"Yes, and you know what we think, my father and I? We guess

that the man who wanted to reward my father, was himself guilty of sin, getting money by false dealings. That is Communist behaviour. Perhaps he wanted to do someone good, to make himself feel better. Long ago his father and mother told him it is very wrong to steal."

"That is very logical thinking. Your father and mother pray, you and they are rewarded."

"With someone's stolen money. God's justice. We are so happy that God looks after us." Paul's smile was infectious.

"I'd call it poetic justice. Great! I must tell Tracy, my wife. She will enjoy that. And, I have an invitation for you, and all your family, to come and have a meal with us, after Danny is well and home again. You deserve it."

"Thank you, Gordon and Tracy. We shall enjoy it very much."

When school closed for the day, Gordon joined Tracy in Danny's room at the hospital. He entered silently and saw Tracy's face light up as she saw him. She stood and motioned him outside the door.

He hugged her and said, "Is he still getting better?"

"Yes, he wakes more often then sleeps again. And we're giving him milk today as well as fluids. I try not to disturb his sleep. I think it's healing. Come and we'll sit together."

They prayed in whispers; "Thank you God. We praise you for healing Danny."

They watched him stir a little. After a little while he stirred again and Tracy touched him gently, saying, "Would you like a drink Danny?"

His eyelids fluttered and Tracy held the cup of milk to his lips. He drank, opened his eyes and gazed at their faces.

"Daddy's here, Danny," said Tracy.

His eyes closed again and slowly, Gordon stood up. "Perhaps I'll leave him to you."

At that moment Danny turned his head and said, "Daddy."

Gordon kneeled beside the bed, saying "Hullo Danny. My brave boy. Daddy loves you," while stroking his forehead.

Gordon and Tracy were beaming while his eyes closed.

An hour later they drove home together, finding Marilyn at their house with Melissa and a casserole cooked for their dinner. At sight of Tracy, Melissa ran to her mother, holding out her arms to be lifted up.

Tracy swung her up saying, "Bless you, Mari. Danny talked to Gordon this afternoon."

"Wonderful!" sang Mari. "He's really on the mend. Thank you Lord! Listen Melissa, your brother's getting well again." She did a little waltz, hugging Melissa with Tracy.

Melissa said, "Danny!"

They laughed and whirled about.

"We have a new friend to celebrate with," said Gordon, "when we find a spare day and time to talk. Just now I guess we have a tired little girl who needs to be fed and put to bed. The Lord be praised."

Later in the evening, with Melissa bathed and in bed, Tracy sat beside Gordon who was sitting marking exercise books. "Have you nearly finished? I'm tired. I'd like to go to bed right now. I'll make a drink of cocoa."

"Right, ten minutes, I'll be with you." By the time Gordon was climbing into bed Tracy was almost asleep, but she stirred as he cuddled her.

"I really want to know more about Paul," she said. "Have you been telling him about Danny?"

"He's a good friend, and the physics teacher. Yes, somehow he knew about my little boy being ill, and first thing he said he would pray for his healing, which surprised me. That was two days ago, and look at our son now! Paul seems to know what he's talking about, since he and his family have been persecuted in Communist

China. They need to do a lot of praying to just survive. It's a God-less country with poor quality of life."

"I feel sorry for them. It makes me shiver just to think of it."

He tightened his arms around her. "Paul is a well-integrated person. You wouldn't think that he and his family have had such hard lives. It's still not easy for them, arriving in a strange country, new language but no money. Paul and his father are very clever as well as loving God. Now Paul has a degree they are sending money back to their families in China, besides working hard here."

"That makes me ashamed. When I get to know them I'll have to see if I can help."

"They will be worth our friendship. They are already receiving help from their church. I'm grateful to Paul now for his prayers and teaching me how to pray."

"That's how I feel about Winifred teaching me, this week. I think we're both different people from a week ago."

On Saturday morning their roles changed. Gordon stayed at home to look after Melissa, while Tracy was at the hospital caring for Danny. Mari, of course, was working, and doing her own preparation. Danny was noticeably brighter, sitting up when offered food such as ice cream and mashed banana. Tracy read to him from his favourite books, including the sea creatures.

"What are they doing now I'm not there to look after them?" he demanded to be told.

Tracy had to use her imagination to tell about the tide coming in, bringing more creatures and nice dinner for the crabs and sea anemones to eat.

He lay back and thought about that and made his own suggestions. After a little nap, when she stroked his face, he woke and said, "There might be a big fish coming in and eating the little ones!"

He was upset until Tracy calmed him by saying that couldn't happen because the water was too shallow for a big fish to swim in.

And so the day passed, and Tracy said, "You'll go to sleep tonight, have a lovely sleep so that you'll feel well tomorrow. Promise me, just think about the crabs and fish having a sleep too."

"All right. Tomorrow I want to go to Grandma's beach."

When the morning arrived, and Tracy's visit to Danny, the nurses reported that indeed he had slept well, and was demanding to go home. "We have to ask the doctor," they said.

And so it was a day of joy and thanksgiving that Danny was allowed to go home for a visit after lunch, and that included a trip to his favourite beach. He insisted on checking his fish pools, and was pleased to see that the rest of the beach was as beautiful as usual. After that he allowed himself to be cajoled inside for a rest.

Tracy and Mari occupied the big arm chairs, each with a child; Danny leaning his head on Grandma's shoulder, while drinking warm chocolate milk. The men came in from the garden and they all chatted happily in this atmosphere of bliss. Mari was counting her blessings.

Monday was another day of happy rejoicing. Tracy again took Melissa to Mari, while saying that it would probably be the last day of this arrangement. "I'll cook again today," said Mari.

"You're wonderful."said Tracy.

"So are you. You'd better hasten now to the hospital, or that boy will be out looking for you."

Paul was also looking out, as the school day passed, to greet Gordon. At lunch time they met gladly, Paul inviting Gordon's company to talk. "Shall we take our coffee with us?" They walked to Paul's room. "Now tell me, how is Danny's progress? Two days of improvement I hope."

"Yes, indeed. That brave little chap insisted on being taken to the beach to check on his precious fish, afraid that they had been damaged in his absence. We had a great day yesterday, though Danny had to go back to his hospital bed last night. It won't be long until he's discharged."

"God be praised. Now you, how are you feeling now?"

"Tracy and I are very relieved, and happy. We feel that this is a learning time for us."

Paul paused thoughtfully. "I have been thinking about you, my friend. I sense that God is at work in your life, and that this distressing illness in your child – no, he doesn't send illness – but now that it has occurred the Lord can bring good out of the unhappy situation. We learn best when trials come into our lives, and the Lord wants you to know how much He loves you. You know, when our lives are going along smoothly we commonly don't think much about God. I think that He's taking this opportunity to teach you about Himself. He loves you so much, extravagantly in fact. His desire is to make each one of us the son or the daughter of God, to purify us, if you like, so that we shall be able, with Him, to enjoy all the blessings He is preparing, while we are living eternally with Jesus Christ."

"That could be mind-blowing. I can't take it in. Why does He bother with us?"

"In one word, Love. I believe that He created us, wanting our company and our love. He tells us, when we read the Bible, a good deal about His desires for us, and about Jesus Christ who came to this world to show and tell us about Father God."

"That's amazing. If He's God He could have made robots to love Him."

"But, He's given us free will. And if we choose to love Him, that gives more value to the love, don't you think?"

"I suppose, yes. My wife chooses to love me, my children also. If they were to direct their love elsewhere, how terribly sad I would be."

"Forgive me for asking, as I know you're a well-educated man, but have you read any part of the Bible for yourself?"

"No, I don't know it. I may have been in church a few times, but none of it has rubbed off on me. I can't say I'm well educated."

"I'd love to hear what you think, if you were to read it, especially the four gospels of the New Testament. May I offer you a loan of this, the New Testament?"

"Where would I begin, anywhere specific?"

"There are four gospels, each one written by a man who lived for three years in the company of Jesus Christ, the Son of God; in one case he drew the information from a close companion of Jesus. We call this Jesus the Son of God; actually He is one part of the Triune God. The everlasting God. He says of Himself, 'My thoughts are high above your thoughts.' It's almost impossible for us to understand. Personally, I feel greatly privileged, now that I am a humble disciple of Jesus, that He sometimes gives me small glimpses of understanding. It's like seeing the unseen, but I'm unable to put it into words. However, there are many people who have seen more wonderful things than I have. The longer we live, communicating with God, seemingly He does reveal more. At times, these revelations come to a person after a period of personal suffering."

"So, can I take it that your loyalty to God brings other-worldly blessings, of value to you?"

"Yes, that is how I see and experience it."

Gordon paused, puzzled. "But why become a martyr, or some-such if you don't have to?"

"That is rational thinking. I'm not surprised that, living here in an affluent, beautiful country you feel like that. You've got freedom as well as those blessings. Compare it with China, mainly poor and oppressed. To us Chinese, the teaching, the words of Jesus give us hope for a better life, here, as a Christian and in eternity."

There was a long pause. Gordon said humbly, "I appreciate

greatly that you've chosen to relieve my ignorance in these matters that you consider very important. I realise that I must read this book, the New Testament, and spend time and thought on it. Thank you."

Tracy had arrived at the hospital, to find an impatient Danny saying, "I want to go home."

Again the answer was, "Wait until the doctor says that you can."

As the doctor was busy elsewhere, the waiting time was endured unwillingly. Tracy persuaded him to lie quietly while she read stories, with the threat of not going at all. Finally he was discharged with another warning about relapse.

"Can we go to Grandma's now?" he insisted.

"Yes, a little short visit, but you're not allowed to run fast along the beach. We're going to pick up Melissa, then we go home quietly."

Mari was, of course, delighted to receive them as was Melissa. The fish were allowed a very quick visit, because, as Tracy said, "other people have work to do. I'll be back to cooking meals and we'll let Grandma have a rest. Thank you so much, Mari, you're an angel."

When Gordon arrived home they had another celebration with an excited Danny.

"I'd appreciate it if you were to encourage Danny to be less energetic," said Tracy, "at least until bedtime this evening."

So Gordon sat with the children while Tracy cooked, wondering how Tracy managed to get her work done on most days. But what a superb burst of energy it was, God be thanked.

Later, while both children were sleeping, Tracy and Gordon sat on a couch together, in grateful happiness. "What have you and Paul been talking about today?" she asked.

"Heaps. A certain amount concerning China, and the ghastly behaviour of the Communist leaders. Much of it is barely credible.

Perhaps they've done a few commendable things, but the rest is a tale of mismanagement, with stupid decisions which cause millions to die of starvation. There is no freedom of speech, with rewards for anyone who will report all and every disloyal word. Corruption and dishonesty thrive among the leaders. Paul tells me that numerous of their relatives have died of starvation. Mao said that a good woman can make a good meal out of nothing, while the officials live in comfort. Even newly born babies have been killed and cut up as meat and sold. Called rabbit!"

"That's sickening! Are there no laws to control that?"

"The police are occupied on more important things I understand. However, conditions may have improved generally now. I certainly hope so. Mao is now deceased and China's doors are more open than previously. Their economy is growing, so let's pray that culturally they are becoming more civilised."

"The Chinese I've met here are really delightful people, so good mannered and kind."

"Like Paul and others I've met. But China is such a vast country. Perhaps the management and the way laws are implemented varies in different towns. Paul stands out as a good, well-educated friend."

"He helped you as Winifred helped me, that day and since then. You know, I felt I was searching for God's help but didn't know how. She immediately seemed to bring me in close touch to Him. I'll never forget the sensations of comfort and warmth. It was like coming home from far away."

"Lucky you. I wish that could happen to me. Paul tells me that he has moments of blessing with God. Look, I'll show you what he's given to me to read." He picked up the New Testament.

"Oh, I've got a Bible somewhere. I did go to church sometimes as a teenager, and we were encouraged to read it. I somehow forgot, but I'll try harder."

"I intend somehow to find the time to do it."

The next day, Mari dialed Tracy's phone. As Tracy answered Mari said, "How's the invalid today?"

"Do you mean the young one? He has the energy of two boys but his mother is about to have a nervous breakdown. A hospital bed would be very welcome to her."

"Oh, I sympathise with you. Would it help to give him a visit to the beach today?"

"Yes, at least a short one when I go out shopping. But I'll try to talk him into having a rest in the afternoon. What I do want to ask is, how about we as a family have a beach picnic on Saturday to make up for what he's lost. Not involving you but while you're working. Once again, keeping our mess out of your house. I can keep it as a treat, a promise if he's good."

"That strikes me as a good idea. While you're here, I thought about inviting Danny to sleep here one night, as he asked a couple of weeks ago. The problem of space for a bed could be solved by letting him camp under Howard's desk. It's so big. You know how kids like to play house, under a table or similar. With a lilo, blankets or a sleeping bag, and a heavy rug to make walls, he might enjoy it."

"I'm sure he'd be delighted. You'd have to protect yourselves, early to bed or you might regret it. You'll be the most loved Granny ever."

Chapter Eight

Dwayne was standing on the footpath, trying to work up his courage to enter the door under the sign 'Alton Electrics'. His mouth was dry, his heart was pounding. A van bearing the same name on the side drove out from the vehicle entrance close by. He said to himself mentally, Get on with it man. The worst is that he'll say no. You've nothing to lose.

At last he took the step to open the door into a small reception room with chairs and a typist at a desk in the corner.

The young woman said, "Good morning sir. Can I help you?"

Dwayne stuttered a little and said, "I'd like to talk to the manager please."

"May I ask your name, sir?"

"I'm Dwayne Jefferson," thinking as he spoke, I wish I had a plain name.

"I'll ask him. He's probably busy." But after the quick phone call she said, "You can go in. I'll show you where to go."

Mr Alton was a worried looking man, early in middle age, who said, "Hullo Dwayne. What can I do for you?"

"I'm an electrician sir. I've recently served my time and I'm looking for a job."

"Is that so? Well, sit down while you show me your papers." Dwayne produced his papers and curriculum vitae. Alton scanned them and said, "You've come a long way from home. Why here?"

"I tried to get a job in Greymouth but there were no vacancies. My mother suggested I come to stay with my aunt who lives here while I look for work."

"What's her name?"

"Mrs Alice Cobbold."

At this, Howard looked up sharply for the first time, noting the tall, thin, nervous young man who stared at his own twitching hands. The paper in his hand read 'Cobbold.' "I thought you said Jefferson." He stared harder. "Cobbold's a dirty word here."

Dwayne looked as though he were ready to cry. "I know sir. I said to my auntie that I wouldn't be welcome here. But I've got good refs and I work hard, very carefully. My boss said he'd trust me, but jobs are scarce and he couldn't afford to keep me on."

Howard looked again at the refs, which were excellent. His own business was going well and he could use a reliable man. "But my staff wouldn't work with a Cobbold. If only you had a different name."

Dwayne looked up beseechingly. "I wish I could change my name." Again he looked ready to cry. "You see, at home I was ashamed of my dad. He was an alcoholic, not a good man. He killed himself, drunk driving. My mum suffered. I want to help her."

Howard, basically a fair man, considered him thoughtfully. "I could send you to a lawyer I know if you'll change your name by deed poll. That would be legal and final. No going back."

"Oh yes, please. I want it to be final. I've hated my father. My mother might change her name too." For the first time Dwayne looked happy.

"There may be a cousin of yours, lurking about here occasionally. He's the son of his father. Keep away from him, absolutely, for your own sake. Keep the name change quiet. Same for your aunt."

"Thank you sir. I'll keep it to myself, absolutely; and tell my aunt. She's suffered too."

"If I take you on, you'll be under a manager, Ted Flaws. I'll be asking for a report from him, continually. Get back to me after the name change. Here's your lawyer's name."

"Thank you sir, very, very much." A beaming young man returned to tell the news to his aunt.

In early evening Howard returned home, to be greeted with savoury smells and his wife in the kitchen, rolling sweet short pastry and complaining quietly over the job.

"Darn," she said. "It won't hold together."

"What are you making?" Howard asked.

"Little fruit tarts for your lunch. We may be poor but we're going to eat well."

"It's nice." Howard picked scraps off the edges of the board.

"Don't eat it raw, silly. You won't get your tarts. You're looking pleased with life. What's happening at work? Going well?'

"Quite well. Construction jobs are doing as they're supposed to in the summer. I'm thinking of hiring a man called Cobbold."

Those words stopped her work. With big eyes she said, "Not really? Are you looking for trouble?"

"It's quite a story. I hope you agree with me. This young chap, painfully nervous, came to me for a job, having just finished his apprentice-ship in Greymouth. Little opportunity of work there, so he came here to live with Aunt Alice Cobbold. Sad story, of two sisters marrying undisciplined losers. I had to tell him I couldn't bring that name into the firm. When he pleaded to get work by changing his name, completely, I agreed on that condition. My business is going well and I can use him. I could see he thought he'd been given a new life."

"The poor lad, a needy case with a rough start. He has every reason to be co-operative and work well. I think you've made the right decision." She stood on her toes to kiss his chin. "You're in line for a halo."

"Well, that's not all," he said, putting another crumb into his mouth. "I've got something to show you if you come into work with me tomorrow. One of the chaps has a small car for sale, if you don't mind it being a bit old. It's a small Toyota with a good motor, well looked-after. It might suit you."

"Oh yes! I'll love it, so long as it's reliable. Darling, I love you." She threw her arms around his neck.

"That's payment for the tarts," he said, kissing her hair.

To herself she thought, Thank you Lord, I do feel sure that you are at work here. That good will come from this, I trust you.

Mari was singing as she drove her neat little car to Winifred's house. I haven't made sure if she's home, but I feel that she is.

Sure enough, Win was out in the sun weeding her garden. The welcome was as warm as she expected. "My darling, you're mobile again! This is your own car! It's a smart little thing. I guess you're happy with it."

"I'm delighted. Howard bought it for me. I feel I've got wings and I can go anywhere. I've got life, abundant and I love it."

Their hug was mutual pleasure.

"Yes, the Lord loves to bless you and to reward you. God is generous to us when we live in the way He desires for us. Loving and praising Him, obedient, enduring, hearing His voice while we rely on His guidance. How's that for a little sermon?" she laughed and so did Mari. "I like it, because that's how you used to make me feel comforted when you were my teacher. It's so pleasant to know when you're doing the right thing."

"I know I can say that to you safely, for you will not pick anything out of it to make you proud of yourself. Some would, but not you. Your mind is big enough to see the whole picture and simply be thankful. Today, you're seeing God at work in your life." She slipped her arm through Mari's and they walked into the house. "Now, coffee or my lemon drink?"

"I do like your lemon drink in warm weather. It's so refreshing."

They made themselves comfortable and Win asked, "How's the little lad?"

"He's a box of birds, and gone to kindy, to Tracy's relief."

"I am so pleased. You can relax somewhat."

"True, but the Lord is doing something in their lives, I do believe. Of course, the fact that you prayed with Tracy; that started a movement, I think, in her life. And, I may have told you that Gordon's co-teacher, his name's Paul, has been brotherly to Gordon. I think that Tracy and Gordon both may be discovering the Lord."

"Wonderful! God be praised! There's often a good start after seeing healing. It's faith-building."

"And I know how good you are at passing on the love of God to someone. It's in your words and everything about you. He is, I should say."

During the high school lunch hour, Gordon was sitting at his desk in the empty class room, reading the New Testament.

Paul, passing his door, greeted him, saying, "How's it going?"

"Great. These stories are very moving. I enjoyed Matthew and Mark, but especially this one, Luke. I'm told he was a doctor, which brings a different light on the story. The details fascinate me."

"I do agree with you. I think I told you that Jesus is a real historical figure, mentioned in historical documents. I know that I have been moved to tears by the treatment He was given."

"But the big question for me is why? How can I comprehend all this, on the one hand the Bible story telling that God, this super-human being who created the universe, and us, plus animals, while the study of physics puts a totally different story of the development of the universe. You, for instance, are highly educated in physics. Do scientists believe in God as creator?"

"Some do so. We have faith in God. God is a Spirit. We have

souls and spirits, and we can communicate, our spirits to His. We commonly look at this world and suppose that what we see is important, and will continue, but actually there is a great unseen spiritual world which will last after this one has crumpled." Paul pulled up one of the hard wooden chairs and sat on it, to face Gordon. "God has foretold that He will create a new heaven and a new earth. There will be a great and fascinating future for us to see, we who are then His sons and daughters. The Bible is a great teaching book for us to learn about God, and how to live, and His commands. He demands obedience. He says that His disciples are to love and praise Him, and be loyal, not giving in to the evil one."

"I'm happy to do that. I believe He is God, and Jesus gives me the redemption to save me."

"Me too. We can't dismiss His statement that He is the Son of God. Either that is true, or this man is an out and out mad-man. If that's all he was, He would have disappeared from history very early. In His love and kindness, Jesus tells us that He goes before us to prepare a place for us. So that's a comfort for us, poor little earthlings that we are."

The clatter of shoes in the corridor and boys loud voices broke their conversation. "I think some more little earthlings have arrived, so we are back to work. See you later."

Dean Jefferson Cameron stood on the pavement, looking at the sign 'Alton Electrics', but this time he did not falter. Instead, he stepped confidently through the door and, with a big smile, asked to see the manager. Once there, he put his papers on Alton's desk, saying, "I've done it, sir."

"Done what?" asked Howard, "Oh, I see. The name. Dean Cameron. Very neat. And you've changed the name on these other papers, with the lawyer witnessing all. Tidy and legal and easy to say. Good work. Come with me now, I'll introduce you to Ted Farrell.

As I said, he's your boss and will report to me. Our firm has a good reputation in this town for reliable work, which you will continue."

"Thank you sir."

Tracy had just finished reading a story to Danny and Melissa in bed. Returning to the living room she found Gordon reading, and asked, "How's your bedtime story?"

"Paul and I have some interesting discussions. With those and reading this New Testament my brain is humming. Sometimes I feel a long way out of my depth. I want to learn more but it must be a vast subject. I suppose you might have to spend your life learning. I'll talk to Paul about how to do it."

"That's a good idea. I'll do something similar with Winifred. If we found a good church, the right teachers would help us. I'll ask Win about books to read."

Marilyn was working in her kitchen when she saw two little girls, pottering on the beach near the rock pools. She was reminded of her resolve to be generous with her time, and offering to teach piano to children who possibly lacked the money and the means. She wandered out to the beach, waving in greeting. "Hullo Sarah," she called. "I see you're interested in the fish pools." Mari's heart warmed to the young, slight girls in their bare feet, pony tails and cotton school uniforms.

Sarah replied politely, "Hullo Mrs Alton. Yes, our teacher said we should do a study of where we live."

"This is a most interesting strip of beach," agreed Mari. "My grandson Danny, he's four, is fascinated by these little creatures. He's reading, or trying to read, a book about sea creatures. I have it here now. Would you like to see it?"

"If he doesn't mind, yes I would." Sarah glanced at her companion, who nodded, a little shyly. "My friend is Kathy."

"Lovely to meet you, Kathy. My name is Mari. Would you both like to come in to see the book?" They followed her into the house, brushing sand off their knees and wiping their feet on the door mat. Child-like, they looked with interest about the room. Mari felt it necessary to explain that she and her husband were living there for only a short time because they had to leave their big house. Kathy broke her silence by asking, "Where do you keep your piano Mrs Mari?" Sarah looked at her friend, a little embarrassed.

"In another house, for the time being," said Mari. "How did you know I have a piano?" She was surprised, then realised that talk had gone about concerning her. "It's all right," she said quickly. "I guess you're interested in pianos. Do you have lessons?"

"No, I wish I did," she mumbled.

"There's a piano at Kathy's house but no one plays it," said Sarah, kindly. "I think she'd like to. I think it belongs to her grandma."

"Is your grandma going to take it back again?"

"I don't think so. She doesn't even play it now. I just wanted to know what it would sound like."

"I think you've come to the right place. When I go to my piano in the other house, I could take you with me in the car. Then you would hear it."

Both girls looked brighter. "That would be nice," they said, nodding.

"You know, Sarah and Kathy, I was wondering if you would like to have piano lessons. But, to learn you would need to have a piano handy, like in your own house. Or, in a close friend's house." She saw both their faces light up, to her own pleasure. "If I were to teach you, it would be done properly, just like my other pupils. I would talk to your parents, and put your names on my list, with your phone numbers. You would each have your own book. You would not have to pay for lessons, not unless your parents really wanted to. You see, I really like to give piano lessons to girls who are keen and practise lots. Would you?" Their sparkling eyes and smiles were very positive answers.

"Oh yes please!" said Kathy.

"That would be lovely, Mrs Alton," from Sarah.

"I would be happy to do this, if you are willing to work hard, and practise every day. After school perhaps, and weekends too. Do you live close?"

They nodded.

"All right. Now, to make this kind of official and proper, I'll talk to your mothers, arrange a time for each, or come together if that suits. Anyway, I can arrange it with you all. Leave your phone numbers and so on. You will buy a book each if your mother approves. Do you like the sound of that? Ask me questions if you like."

Two happy children went off home with smiling faces after some chat. Mari returned to her kitchen, thinking gratitude to the Lord for organising the fulfilment of her desires. She remembered clearly her own happy days of learning.

Another lunch hour, and Paul put his head around Gordon's door, saying, "Hi mate, how goes it?"

"Still struggling along. What's bugging me is that so many people have different ideas about God, if they think about Him at all, that is. I wish you would tell me what you think, as you seem to be acquainted with Him, and you are educated, I mean. The laws of nature, as we call physics."

"I believe personally that God invented physics, then probably left it for us to find. He wants us to use our brains. As for the Genesis story, it's an excellent introduction written probably by Moses to teach a tribe of not highly educated people about their origins. Perhaps some might have met physics. We don't know. But God had very personal reasons for wanting to teach this tribe, Israel, about Himself. He loved them, He wanted to have a love relationship with them, and He wanted them to be an example to the rest of the world in how to live; to have Godly, clean lives, healthy in their habits, decent to one another, that is, loving. Let's face it, we wouldn't have found their lifestyles comfortable or safe, on the whole. Worse still, there was existing already a strong, evil person named Satan. His main desire was to wreck God's world by sinful behaviour which would have ruined God's plan to have a happy-forever future with God's prime creation in eternal life. So the humans were in desperate need of being cleaned up, made decent livable people. God gave Moses the ten commandments to teach the people how to live, without destroying one another, and to recognise sin. The penalty for sin is death. A harsh penalty, but compare it with the rewards God gives us for serving Him. Eternal life in paradise with God."

After a pause, Gordon took a deep breath and said slowly, "I really appreciate that, the way you explain it to sound almost simple. But it can't be, can it? I guess that all the words in the Bible are there because they have to be."

"You're right. Christianity is a very complex study, and much of it can only be learned by our spirit, from God's Spirit. This overview of the Old Testament shows the need for God to send a special Person who is part of God, to teach men about God and His amazing love. In the Old Testament God taught the priests and the people to offer a sacrifice, a perfect lamb, to show repentance for their sins. A ritual offering. But later, the perfect sinless Jesus came to be the sacrificial Lamb. He was killed, voluntarily carrying the sins of everyone in the world. And so we benefit when we choose to take Jesus into our lives; in fact to surrender to Him. The grace that gives us that amazing, wonderful redemption was not cheap. Therefore we love Him."

"I understand. I thank you mightily, Paul. You are a gifted preacher."

"No more than many others. We all have the Bible and a brain to make use of. Unfortunately some people forget to use it. We need to ask God for help to understand it. I often study a book by CS Lewis. He was a great teacher. The name of the book is *Mere Christianity*. Interestingly, though he wrote many books, the Narnia series are the ones by which millions of people identify him. Their spiritual quality is exceptional. *The Lion, the Witch and the Wardrobe* portrays God's redemption, in a story which is easily understood by children. By the way, God's plan for the redemption of the unhappy inhabitants of this planet, who have and are suffering from the damage done by Satan, is the subject of very large portions of the Bible."

"You've been an outstanding teacher in relieving my ignorance, thank you Paul."

"It is my pleasure. I love the Lord so much. If you wish, I'll lend my books to you."

"Hullo Winifred, it's Tracy here. Yes, thank you, Danny is completely recovered. I wonder if you might recommend some books to me, and Gordon, that will help us to study the Bible and know God better."

"That's a question I'm delighted to answer. Yes, I have some I will show you, to lend you, but also, how about we go together to the book shop. We'll look and ask questions. I'm thinking particularly about an assortment, including a small book of daily readings which a husband and wife can read together. It's important that you can fit it easily into your busy lives, and while you're caring for your children. Also, you can ask about children's books which can be good bedtime reading."

"What a good idea. Yes, can we go one morning while Danny's at kindy? I can think better without his questions."

"There's nothing I'd like better. We'll plan it for the morning."

"Hullo Paul, have you time to stop and talk?"

"Of course, shall we sit here for a few minutes?"

"You know that *Mere Christianity* book you lent to me? I couldn't stop reading it last night. Tracy was reading it over my shoulder, after the kids went to bed. It's super excellent isn't it. No wonder the BBC paid Lewis to speak to the nation back then, to teach the Brits something like a solid foundation. In wartime they certainly needed something and Someone to put their faith into. I'd guess that a few million people must have been driven into praying at that desperate time."

"Indeed, as were my family and I, when we were under Communism. But I do know that in China there has been a great increase in the number of converts to Christianity, even so. Suffering people are drawn to the love of God and the warmth of fellowship associated with Christians."

"Speaking of which," said Gordon, "Tracy and I are considering the idea of finding a good church which will help us to grow as God would have us do. I've been sensing that God wants me, wants us to learn more about Him. Would you think we'd find what we're looking for at your church?"

"That I can't say for certain, but we are a mixture of people without pride; some of us have had difficult lives, we're grateful for all that the Lord gives us and we're sincere in our approach to God. Our pastor is an aging, well taught in the Bible, and experienced minister. As well as that he has compassion and humility. We have love for one another."

"With all those qualities it surely is a good church. What more could we ask for?"

"We'd like to welcome you as a family. There's a Sunday school for children four years and up, and a pleasant little crèche for babies. Two to three years have toys. Sometimes we have very good teaching sessions."

"Really! I could be interested. On what subject?"

"Various. Soon we'll have some on science; Professor Jeffrey Tallon, professor of physics at Victoria University. He's recognised by the academic world, including Cambridge University. He'll be talking on cosmology and the Bible."

"Heavy stuff! I'd love to hear him. May I come?"

"Of course. Your wife might be interested too."

Mari was enjoying the morning of sunshine, the songs of nesting birds and, overall, the presence and atmosphere of the living sea breathing in its turquoise bed. While weeding and tying up the vigorous green shoots of tomatoes she felt utter contentment, until the crackle of car wheels on the gravel road. A little annoyed, she dropped her tools, to investigate the strange car. An unfamiliar, middle aged lady approached her. Puzzled, she stared, then surprised, recognised Mrs Cobbold. Hastily she arranged a smile on her face and said, "How lovely to see you, Mrs Cobbold. Such a long time since we met. Come in, we'll sit down and catch up on how life's treating you."

Mrs C clasped Mari's hand and allowed herself to be led inside. She sat, and while Mari apologised for her dirty hands and washed, Mrs C looked about the room and its very modest furnishings. She said, "My dear, I am sorry to see that you've had to come to this."

Mari sought a suitable reply and came up with a smile, saying, "It's really very nice living in a small house close to the beach. Quite like a holiday. Now, can I make you tea or coffee?"

They progressed with polite nothings until, with the coffee and biscuits on the table, Mrs C came to the reason for her visit. "I've been longing to apologise for a long time. Things have been rather difficult for me too, for I've come near to having to leave my own home. To say nothing about the shame of my husband breaking up the business. I don't dare to face people now. I feel like an outcast."

"Yes, I can imagine that," said Mari feelingly.

"Well now, I hope to make a little reparation, how small I'm not sure. But there is a race horse, legally half mine now. I desperately want to sell it, to break away from that life. But I'll have to fight with those horsey types, to get it done. They are not anxious to pay out to me, as you'd expect."

"Yes, I can commiserate with you," said Mari, thinking how difficult life is.

"Yes, I don't know how much it will be worth to me, some thousand I would expect. Whatever, that must belong to your firm; your husband."

Mari was aware of some singing in her brain, a joyful song. Don't get excited too soon she was telling herself.

But Mrs C was still speaking. "I know your husband has given a job to my nephew, for which I'm so grateful. I know Dean's changed his name; who wouldn't want to? So I keep quiet about it. He is a good boy, trustworthy. I hope he does well."

"I expect he will work well and be an asset to us. Having difficulties can often stimulate to apply harder to be a success. I'm sure your support is very helpful to him."

"I hope so. He is a try-er, and loves to have a bit of praise. He's helping me with my garden." She glanced out towards Mari's garden. "Perhaps you could do with some help, at this time of year?"

"Oh, yes. I would really appreciate that. Send him along, whenever he's willing. I'm busy, teaching piano. Howard doesn't have time to spare."

"I am pleased to give you a hand. Now, I don't want to go into the office and be recognised by the staff. I want, some day, to make a transfer of money to the firm privately. Could you give me the necessary information, bank numbers and so on?"

Mari leaped to her feet and opened Howard's desk. "I'll make a list and find you a document or two." She searched. "Here you are. Do you think that's sufficient?"

"Probably. I'll give these to my lawyer." She rose to her feet. "As I said, I'm so sorry that you and your husband have suffered through this. But I am impressed that you are coping so well."

Wryly, Mari said, "It has been and still is rather difficult. But we battle on." They walked out to the car. "We both appreciate your offer of help. I feel for you. It must have been painful."

"Yes, quite dreadful. I'll feel a little happier if I can repay somewhat. Thank you for your tolerance. Goodbye my dear."

Mari lost no time in ringing Winifred. "You'll never guess what's happened, Win dear. Mrs Cobbold," and she poured out the tale, finishing with the chances of the sale not going through.

Win laughed at that. "Such a minor thing to the Lord. She'll have a surprise when it happens."

"Did I tell you about Mrs C's nephew? About Howard giving him a job after he changed his name from Cobbold?"

"I don't think so."

Mari told the story of the unfortunate young man's inclusion in the Alton firm. "And keep it a secret because the other staff wouldn't work with a Cobbold."

"Well, that's a story worth hearing. So Auntie's grateful in coming up with her offer!"

"Yes. And she's promised me that he'll help me with my garden."

"Praise be! That's sounds like God's way of doing things."

Chapter Nine

Mari and Howard had their usual busy weekend until Sunday afternoon, when Tracy phoned to ask if it was all right to come visiting. "I've cooked something tasty which I'll bring for our tea."

"Bless you, Tracy, you're always welcome, without bringing food. Thank you, it'll be lovely."

They arrived shortly after, Danny bursting out of the car to visit his fish first. Tracy called him back to greet his grandparents. After hugs and kisses, Mari invited them in, and Tracy explained that Melissa was still a little sleepy. "Her sleep was later today because we've been to church and Sunday school."

"Oh, do tell me about it," said Mari.

Danny had immediately gone to look at his fish.

"You tell, Gordon, you know them a little better," said Tracy.

"I haven't experienced church services so I wouldn't know how to compare with any other. But my respect for Paul Chang made me expect something of good quality, and I think it was. The welcome as we stepped inside was sincerely warm. The singing was good, with guitars and a few other instruments, and what I would call enthusiasm. The man who gave the sermon impressed me; he was easy to listen to while keeping everyone awake. He spoke as though knowing God well, as Paul does. But before the sermon the children streamed out of the back door for their Sunday school,

Danny with them. You can ask him. I'm sure the answer will be positive."

"I'm sure he enjoyed it," said Tracy. "And they invited us to stay for a shared lunch! Think of that. We met Paul's family, and they are really charming people. They introduced us to their friends, but I said we really had to get Melissa home for a sleep. There will be more things I'll look forward to sharing with them."

"That's wonderful. I feel that the Lord is leading you. You are on the right path."

"We certainly shall have more fascinating topics to stretch our brains. Paul tells me that on a Sunday evening very soon, I think it will be two weeks from now, there will be a guest speaker, name of Professor Jeffrey Tallon, coming to the town to one of the big churches, for which others may combine. Personally I'm delighted, because he's the Professor of Physics at Victoria University. His work has received many awards. He's lectured at Cambridge University. Also, he's a Christian, believes that God is active in creation. The Bible is God's book to tell us ordinary people what the scientists have been learning. They write it as strings of equations; the history of the growth of the universe. They are totally amazed. Our planet, and we who live on it, almost didn't happen."

"But what good will this lecture be to us, the ignorant hoi-poloi?" asked Tracy.

"We'll find it interesting to hear that now the scientists have uncovered so many details of what has happened in the 300 million years that have gone by since the big bang happened, changes in the minutest details which, if they had been the faintest bit different at those times, would have prevented our planet from forming and we would not be here. And that implies that a good designer was in control."

Howard had been listening intently, and now said, "I think this is something important that would enliven our brains. The very little that I learned about electricity was just enough to make me wish that I knew more, as you have gone on."

"Thanks Dad, for helping me to be where I am."

Mari was smiling with enthusiasm. "I'm glad you've told us this, Gordon, because I'm thirsty to know more. I'm ignorant and may not be able to understand it, but I want to know all I can."

"Yes, me too," said Tracy. Gordon was looking at her with approval.

"Stretching our brains is always a good thing," he said. "Paul is more educated than I am, and it shows in the way he talks. I respect him for the way he is coping in a new country, after being bullied by the Communists in China."

"I do too," said Tracy. "I thought there was real strength, a spiritual growth in that church today." She was sitting in an arm chair with a sleepy Melissa on her lap.

At that moment Danny rushed in, forgetting to wipe his feet, and showed Gordon a piece of wet brown seaweed with a minute creature on it. "Look Daddy, it's a different one! I think it might be a baby one."

There were smiles all round from the proud parents. "Congratulations Danny! You're learning to be a scientist." He absorbed the praise, as his due.

"I'll help you with reading that book about sea creatures Danny, if you would like me to. There are so many big words in it, I'll have to learn them too," said Howard in his approving voice. So Danny found the book and they sat at the table together, quietly talking.

Tracy told Mari about meeting Paul's mother and father. "I can see in their faces that they've had a hard life. But they have beautiful personalities, not at all sorry for themselves. I admire the whole family."

"I am looking forward to meeting and getting to know them, if they will allow that. They'll be far different from our previous friends, that's for sure."

After Gordon and his family had left for home, Mari said to Howard, "I haven't told you about Mrs Cobbold visiting me the other day."

He looked up from his book in surprise. "Really? Why?"

"She came to me instead of you because she didn't want the office staff to recognise her. She wanted to apologise to us, for what happened. In fact, she wants to make some restitution to the firm."

Howard dropped his glasses and gazed at Mari, open mouthed. "But people just don't do things like that!"

"I know. But she said it. Apparently there is still a race horse, half owned by her. She is saying that it will be justice if our money, stolen to buy that horse, is returned to us."

"Hmm. If her heart is sure about doing the fair thing, there might still be difficulties about the outcome." His half smile showed that he liked the thought. "Or if the horse is worth it, and if everyone concerned is kind and honest."

"I know, there may be any number of imps who would try to sabotage a good deed. But I have friends who will have strength from another source." Howard looked at her quizzically but was quiet. "And, besides, I have something I'd like to suggest. I don't suppose you have found the boundaries for our section here?"

Howard shook his head.

"Well, I think it would be a good idea to think about it soon. Sylvia's Ben has a promising plan ready to be put on this piece of land. We might be ready to build sooner than you think."

Howard raised his eyebrows a little and looked doubtful. "That sounds as though you know something that I don't."

"Of course I don't know, but I have hopes. I'd love to plan a garden, and thinking of trees, they will be future, and I need to know where I may plant them, in advance."

Howard groaned. "I have an awful feeling that I'll be called in to help."

"Well, I think I might have a helper, with luck. Mrs C said that her nephew liked to help in the garden, and he may come to give me a hand at times."

"Phew, that's a relief. He's doing good work I'm told. We'd better be nice to him."

Mari leaned over to kiss him. "You're always nice to people. That's why I married you."

"I'd love to have a quick visit with you, Winifred, if you have a little time to spare."

"Of course, darling girl, I'll expect you in a few minutes. I'll have the kettle on."

Mari, in her little car, flew on wings of happiness, to the open door.

"This is lovely, Win. I do enjoy being mothered." She relaxed and bit into a muffin.

"As I enjoy you being here. Tell me about everyone."

"We're all okay. You'd enjoy hearing Gordon talk about his discussions with Paul Chang. They all went to Paul's church on Sunday, and found it stimulating and very welcoming. Danny apparently enjoyed Sunday school. They'll repeat the visit next week."

"Praise be! I love to hear all this. When people begin to walk with the Lord, and they have really good quality fellowship, I'm sure that Jesus' heart is pleased. That's what He came to achieve."

"Yes, isn't it wonderful. I shall try to get there next Sunday. I'm looking forward to meeting Paul and his parents. I hear that they have the most admirable qualities."

"It will be a privilege to meet, and hopefully get to know them. Their experiences must be exceptional."

"And there's more to tell. You know Gordon is a mathematician. He respects Paul the physics teacher. There's a little excitement now, because a very learned and quite famous professor of physics, Professor Jeffrey Tallon, will be speaking in the town two Sunday nights from now. A committed Christian, speaking on the birth of our universe and how it relates to our Bible."

Mari noticed that Win's expression dulled. "I wish I were not so ignorant. I just have to accept what's written in the Bible. It's not of use to me to know anything else."

"But the educated physicist, also a Christian, says that we are pleasing God by learning the mathematics which He invented. I can't do the math either, but I can believe these many scientists who have worked for untold hours on tracing the records of the development of our universe, and this little planet, prepared for us, God's people to inhabit. We don't know of any other habitable planet. The early scientists, from about 300 years ago, started by searching the Bible, inspired by it's insistence of truth, and continuing their endless observations, checking and rechecking."

She spoke with such passion that Win caught her enthusiasm. "Mari, my dear, you sound quite knowledgeable, which shouldn't surprise me, because I always was aware that you could pick things up in record time. How did you learn this?"

"By reading, after Gordon began to tell us what Paul told him. You've heard me talk about Paul, the physics teacher, and their church where Gordon and Tracy went last Sunday. So now I'm telling you about this excellent scientist who will be speaking at one of the mainline churches here. He, and some of the other very intelligent physicists, believe in God and Jesus' offer of salvation. They recognise the fact that no one knows exactly how life began on earth. They believe that God created, they don't know how. Any other theory, like Darwin's little things crawling out of a swamp, has never been proved. Atheists like to pretend to believe it, because they want God out of the picture. Pride is behind that."

"I find that fact, about pride having a motive there, easy to believe. Satan's tactics are to tell men that they do not need God, because Satan's weakness is pride, and he wants to alienate us from

God. Nasty." They held a thoughtful pause. "You've given me an excellent summary, Mari darling. Yes, I am convinced that it would be good to hear this speaker who is doing God's work. Thank you for coming to tell me."

It was a wet afternoon, uncommon for summer. Paul, shaking the rain off his face, pedalled home after school, and was surprised to see a tradesman's van parked outside the house. The sign on it read 'Alton Electrics.' On reaching the back door he dropped his bike and entered, grabbing a towel to dry his head and face.

Inside he met the owner of the van, a tall young man with his electrical tools spread on the bench. He looked up and said, politely, "I'm sorry sir, I'll be finished very shortly and then out of your way."

Paul smiled and said in a friendly voice, "That's all right. Your work is more important than mine. By the way, I'm Paul, a school teacher. My work's just finished for the day."

Dean put down his screw driver and, holding out his hand, said "I'm Dean. I work for Mr Alton."

"I see that. I know Gordon Alton, the son of your boss I suppose?

"Yes. Mr Alton is a very good boss. I'm grateful to him for giving me a job here. I come from Greymouth; I couldn't get a job there. This rain makes me feel like I'm home."

"I don't know that area. I come from China. You can hear my accent." Paul sensed a hesitation in Dean, almost a slight humility, and wondered what was behind it. Dean found himself liking Paul; his pleasant manner and the careful English. "Do you mind if I watch you working, Dean? I'm fascinated by the skill that safely handles electricity."

"If you like, sir."

"Call me Paul."

Ten minutes passed in friendly question and answer.

"You do know something about it, Paul, I can tell," said Dean.

"Most people are scared if I tell them how much electricity is in our surroundings."

"That's what I notice too. When I talk about my subjects, which are physics and cosmology, the mention of radioactive material has people worried."

"Wow! Cosmology is heavy stuff. I'd like to know more about the beginning of the universe."

"It surely is engrossing stuff, and scientists have uncovered a lot more in recent years. You might like to know, there's a major professor coming to this town very soon. I'll tell you where to hear him. You might like to come with me." While talking, Paul had been thinking of how to befriend this young man whom he sensed as being lonely.

It seemed he was right. Dean smiled for the first time. "Yeah, I'd like to. I don't know many people here, only my aunt."

Paul was struck by a sudden idea of how to offer friendship. "I wonder if you might help me to fix a radio that's been given to me. This radio sort of goes, but it's not as good as it should be. I'll pay you for improving it."

"That's all right, I'll be pleased to help if I can." He glanced at his watch. "Time for me to be getting the van back. I can take your radio with me."

They parted company with promises to be in touch.

Mari, standing at her kitchen window, was watching Danny doing his beach work, as he called it, when she saw Sarah, in bare feet and school frock, running along the beach. She stopped to talk to Danny. Mari felt drawn to have a little conversation.

Running to the beach, she called out, "Hullo my darlings. How are the fish, Danny? And how are you getting on, Sarah? Is Kathy enjoying her practice?"

"Oh yes. I've been to her place today. We take turns and it's fun.

Did you know that she used to try to play before she had lessons but her dad was cross with her; said it was a messy noise."

"But it's better now I hope?"

"Yes, she sounds much better. Even he can tell the difference." Sarah was quiet and looked somewhat sad.

"What are you thinking, Sarah?"

"Well, I'm sort of worried about Kathy. Her family often say things to each other that are not kind. I'm worried that Kathy is not happy."

Mari hesitated. Is it my business, she was asking herself. Or can I do anything anyway? "Do you think we can do anything to help her, Sarah?"

"I don't know. Well, I can't change anyone, can I, and the only person I can talk to is you. I can't say anything to Kathy or her family. I don't want to upset her any more."

"Is there a counsellor at your school, Sarah? I mean, is there a person you can go to for help if you're in bad trouble, a person who has been trained specially for that?"

Sarah was quiet, rubbing her hair. "I don't think so."

"You've been a very good friend to Kathy, Sarah dear. I'll ask a few people I know, to find out, but without making a fuss. We don't want to upset her more. Bless you dear, you're what we call a friend in need. You're doing well."

"Hullo Win dear, this is Mari again, asking for help. Sarah, my new pupil, is worried about her friend Kathy's state of mind, so I'm wondering if school children have access to a counsellor."

"I'd guess that only a teacher can tell you that. Is it something serious, or potentially so? What about the mother? Do you know her, or the family?"

"No, I'm only the child's music teacher. I've only spoken to the mother on the phone. Just an outsider, you could say."

"Sometimes, Mari, an outsider notices little things that need to be queried, as symptoms which are glossed over by parents, and are indicative of a serious fault. It's easy to pass by and do nothing, but more difficult to be the good Samaritan who helps. It happens all over the world. I would say, follow your instinct and speak to the school teacher. She also has responsibility and some power to ask for help."

"Thank you, Winifred, I think you're right. There must be many kids who need help."

Mari had discovered the name of Kathy's school teacher, thanks to Sarah. And so, after warning Sarah to keep it a secret, she wrote this letter:

Dear Mrs Bennett, I apologise if this seems like an outsider butting in. My name is Mari Alton, a music teacher to Kathy Spencer, who is, I believe, a student in your class. My informant is Sarah , also in your class and a friend of Kathy. Sarah seems to me to be trustworthy. She is very worried about her friend Kathy, whom she thinks is uneasy to a serious level, while living in that family. She appears to be showing depression, unease and withdrawal. The fact is that several family members in that house are showing hostility to one another quite frequently, and often in the presence of Sarah. It appears that Kathy, the youngest, is often the butt of harsh words. I have noticed moments of withdrawal and even fear in Kathy, though she says she enjoys learning the piano and obviously enjoys the praise I give her. I can only leave these impressions with you, Mrs Bennett, because of Sarah's concern.

Yours faithfully, Marilyn Alton, LTCL

When Howard arrived home, Mari sat him down with dinner and soon after decided to run the letter past him, with the story. "Have I done the right thing?" she asked him.

"Well, I wouldn't know. If things there are not good for the child, the teacher is the only other one you can contact. You feel strongly about her, I gather. It's better to raise an alarm than let injustice go on for a young child."

"That's more or less what Winifred said to me. So that's three of us. Darling husband, have you given any thought to the survey for our section?"

"Darling wife, I have. I knew that you would be on my back. He's coming one day this week. Satisfied?"

"Of course. I knew you would. I simply can't stop thinking about what trees can go where."

Mrs Bennett was surprised when Sarah (such a nice girl) handed her the letter. Later, on opening it, she was more surprised. Have I really missed anything, she wondered, a little guiltily. The thought worried her at times, but she was aware that one quiet, well-behaved girl could be overlooked in a class of thirty, many of whom were noisy, disobedient and demanding of her time.

It was not until the end of the day that she was able to show the letter to the headmaster. He questioned her on her observations of the class. "Her work has not changed, that I notice. But perhaps sometimes she does look rather withdrawn. She is a quiet person, normally. There have been times when the kids have to come up with money to pay for something special and there was a delay."

"I would suppose that's a common occurrence in families. But does it suggest a real shortage of cash in that family, and is the cause a serious issue to be considered?" The headmaster mulled these thoughts in his brain. "There are a group of counsellors attached to the university who look into school children who are at risk. She's not an obvious case. Of course, the difficulty is how to investigate without making the child or the mother embarrassed. Should we wait for some other warning sign to appear? I might phone those counsellors for a start. We'll talk about this tomorrow."

Mari was feeling cheerful. It was a fine day and the fattening lettuces and fruit in her garden were a cause for singing. To top off her mood a phone call from Sylvia made her day. She was happy to tell her mother that, having started a new job, it was going well. "It's a private school for girls, quite a cushy job really, hours nine to three thirty."

"So plenty of time to cook your husband's dinner and make a fuss of him. I'd bet he appreciates that."

"Indeed, as you say. He often works some part of the evening, and apparently my humble and uneducated opinion has some value for him."

"He's lucky to have a wife like you to build up his self esteem."

"Well, I do enjoy looking and I'm truly interested. Which brings me to say, how would you like us to visit you and Daddy and show you the special plan he's drawn for you?"

"Oh, lovely. On a day when we're both home in the evening. P'raps a Friday?"

"I'll suggest that to him. Do you know your section size?"

"We should know by Friday. I'm longing to know it. I want to plan my garden. I'm hoping and believing that our house will happen."

Dressed in school uniform, with her lunch box in her hand, Kathy said, "Mum, I need the bus money please. You know we're going to Rotorua today." She already had a nasty feeling somewhere near her stomach because the atmosphere last night had been unpleasant.

Now her mother said only, "I haven't any money. Your father didn't give me any house keeping money last night."

Kathy remembered his angry voice. It was useless to say more. He had left early for his work (he was self employed) saying, "I'll be away part of the day."

Kathy guessed that he might be going to Hamilton for a race meeting. She felt helpless. What could she say when Sarah called to meet her on the way to school? She went to the back door and said, "Bye Mum," then disappeared in the direction of the trees at the back of the house. She couldn't stop the tears from rolling down her face. All the children had been looking forward to this day trip to the new science museum at Rotorua. How embarrassing it would be to tell Sarah or anyone.

Mari was again in her kitchen, keeping a watch on Danny having his play time on the beach. Then she saw Kathy talking to him, but there was no sign of Sarah. That was strange, for they usually did their piano practice at this time of day. A little later, when she looked again, Sarah had appeared and they were talking. As if to check on Danny, Mari went out to say hullo. They all appeared as normal.

After Mari took Danny home, Sarah turned to Kathy. "Are you okay, Kathy? I missed you today. Your mother said you had gone to school."

"I just slept in. When I woke up it was too late to catch the bus. So I stayed home."

Sarah looked at her doubtfully. This story just didn't hang together. But she didn't want to appear curious or embarrass Kathy. "Shall we go and practise now? I haven't done any today. It's getting late."

"All right, let's hurry." They set off at a trot.

On the way Sarah reminded Kathy about Sunday. "I asked Mum and it's all fixed. You're coming with us to church and to lunch after."

Kathy's smile was pure pleasure. "I'll like that. Thank you so much."

On Friday afternoon Mari phoned Winifred. "I'm feeling excited about talking to Ben about the house plan he's offering us. He and Sylvia will come this evening. Howard might think I'm being foolish, at this stage, because we might not build for years and years. But I have a feeling, a sort of an inkling that things might get underway sooner. One fact is that Ben says it's the right type for our situation, and we'll be getting the plan free, or nearly so."

"I feel for you, Mari darling. I can just imagine the excitement. You have a hope that the Lord has given you, that's for sure. Be prepared to wait a bit though, as you know it's a long process. I am still praying that the lady's offer of restitution goes through quickly. But it's right to keep your hope in God's provision. He can be trusted."

"Yes, I'm sure He can. Do you remember the little girl, Kathy, that I said I was worrying about? A strange thing happened yesterday. The class, with Sarah and Kathy were to have a day trip to Rotorua, an important one by bus. But Kathy just didn't turn up for it, then later she was here on the beach talking to Danny. Sarah arrived at the usual time. They talked then walked away together. I'd like to ask Sarah what had happened."

"That sounds to me a sensible idea. It seems to me a fishy situation. There was already a sign of possible trouble. As Sarah has confidence in you, you are in the right place to help a girl who needs it. You've already written a letter; now you can follow up. Bless you Mari dear. I'm still praying for you, and them."

The summer evening was delightful with a faint breeze and setting sun, in tune with Mari's mood. She walked about the area, now called her garden, with the surveyor pegs in place. She had purchased string which now she attached to the pegs, heightened by broom sticks. Her heart was singing as she imagined the picture of trees and flower beds. I know I ought to be tidying the kitchen and preparing for tomorrow's day out. But the arrival of Ben with Sylvia and the house plans brought Howard out to welcome them.

Mari was almost stuttering with excitement, as they entered the kitchen to gather around the table. Ben unrolled the plans. At first it was difficult to relate the drawings to the ground as they saw it outside their walls. But a prolonged walk outside with tape measures helped the pictures to take form in their minds. Ben was full of praise to Howard for buying such an excellent site.

"It was my idea first!" said Mari.

"And my money," said Howard.

Sylvia said, "You watch out to be sure that the kitchen is placed where you want it to be, Mum. These men sometimes do impractical plans. It's important for you to be happy in it, enough sun at the time you want it, as well as convenient for you."

"Yes, I am going to look again at this plan with all that in mind. Do you know what I'd like to do now? I want Jake to come and look at this now."

"A bit early for that, isn't it?" said Howard. "We don't know when, or where the money's coming from."

"Well we would prefer Jake, wouldn't you? I trust his good sense and experience from now on."

So the result was a phone call to Jake who arrived a few minutes later, full of interest. After introductions he put on his glasses. "Hmm. An attractive layout. I guess you've checked the markers for size. D'you mind if I go out to have another look?" He led the way out, remarking, "Your garden's doing well, Mari." She trailed behind him happily. As expected, his comments were practical, and his conversation with Ben was agreeably warm. The sunset clouds were like a blessing from the skies.

As they re-entered the little house Jake said to Howard, "Are you people likely to be wintering in this bach? If you are, you could be warmer if you put some larger second-hand glazing into this north wall. It's very cheap in builder's supplies, discarded by people who have re-glazed. You'd have a warmer house for next to nothing. Not difficult. I could do it in a weekend, with your help."

Their thanks for this suggestion were profuse. As he departed Jake said,"Thanks for your music lessons to Sarah, Mari. She's over the moon about it."

"It's a pleasure," said Mari. "She's a delight to teach."

After the departure of the others, Mari made a phone call to Sarah on her own account. Something was bothering her mind, and only Sarah could answer her question.

The surprised girl told her, "Yes, Kathy said she didn't come on the trip because she slept late. But her mother said she went to school. I don't know who to believe."

Mari said, "You're a good girl Sarah. You are in a team with me while we try to help Kathy. I'm really worried, for her sake. This incident does not sound healthy. I'm planning to tell your teacher. So, not a word to anyone. Bless you, darling."

On Saturday, while Mari was much occupied in teaching her pupils, Dean was loading Paul's radio into the car borrowed from his aunt. Returning it improved was a pleasure, for he was somehow drawn to this family of refugees who worked so hard against a punishing world. Indeed, on his arrival at their house, both father and son came out to welcome him.

"This is Luke Chang, my father," introduced Paul.

They shook hands, asking about his health and offering refreshments.

What charming people, thought Dean, comparing them with his own father. How had Communism taken a hold in such a civilised nation? He knew little of the dreadful history of China.

But after some very pleasant exchanges of conversation, the gritty realities were mentioned. Dean could only feel gratitude for the friendship of these heroic people. Paul mentioned how Dean was also interested in the study of cosmology.

Luke spoke of his own desire for learning, and his pleasure in seeing his sons enjoying a rich education. "In China we respect knowledge greatly. Or we did, until the wretched wars broke down our civilisation. Then Communism destroyed much of what was left." There was a sad silence.

Paul spoke again of the forthcoming lectures about cosmology and its link with the Christian Bible. "Would you like to come with us, Dean? There are an interesting mix of people, and sure to be some you would like. We are a very hospitable crowd. I invite you to come to our church tomorrow, and stay for a shared lunch."

"Thank you, I accept that invitation with pleasure."

Chapter Ten

When Sunday evening arrived Marilyn was still very concerned about Kathy, and made a phone call to Sarah.

While waiting for Sarah's voice, she was worried that she might be asking too much of her. Had Kathy been with Sarah today? Am I being too nosy? But, thank goodness, Sarah was easy and comfortable with this checking.

After Mari put her question, Sarah told her of her own doubts. "Yes, she came to our Sunday school, and I dared to ask her if things were all right on Thursday, because we were very worried about her. She didn't want to say anything so I pushed it. Then she kind of hung her head and told me they didn't have enough money for the bus fare. I told her we could have paid it, and we wanted to help her. I hugged her and she cried a little bit, and said, 'It's my father. He spends money on horse racing. Some times he loses instead of winning.' That's what happened. He had nothing to give Mum."

"Oh, Sarah, how awful for her. She must have been terribly embarrassed. Thank you for telling me. You're a treasure and a good friend. Now we know some facts we can tell the school, privately, and the teachers can arrange some special funding. After I talk to them, they will look after Kathy and you can tell her she won't have that sort of trouble again. I'll do it on Monday."

On Monday Marilyn lost no time in writing a note to Mrs Bennett, to tell her of Kathy's loss of the school trip and the reason. It's so disappointing, she mourned. I feel that now Kathy's mother might be open to receiving counselling for this sad situation.

Mari delivered the letter to the school by hand, thinking of what had been told her about the good Samaritan. He kept his eyes open and took time to give help. Please Lord, be a saviour to this child Kathy. I hope she enjoyed a Sunday with Sarah.

"Marilyn dear, how good of you to ring and tell me about the little girl Kathy. Yes, I have been praying. Your friendship with Sarah is productive and you are doing everything right. And yes; I believe you said the correct thing, that the school would carry the burden of extra expenses in some cases of need. In that way, Kathy's load will be lightened. The unfortunate children in her position often feel obliged to take the parent's mistakes on their own shoulders."

"I'm grateful to you, dear Win, for assuring me of that. I was feeling in the dark, and hoping to get it right. Now, I'm wondering what next I could do. Should I visit Mrs Spencer? Would I be pushing too far; would it help her?"

"You are the child's music teacher, and so it will be a kind and natural thing to tell her how well the pupil is doing. I feel sure she would be pleased and heartened to be told. On the way, she will appreciate having you for a friend. In her position I guess she feels lonely for good friends, which you will be."

"Yes, I feel that's right, now you say it. And while I'm there I may learn how to pray for her. Would you join with me in praying for her, please Win?"

"Of course, with pleasure. On that subject, I know you have a busy life, but how do you feel about meeting, we two together, say once a week, to pray for the Spencer family, as well as whoever seems to be in need?"

"Oh yes, I'd love to. Being with you seems to strengthen my faith in God."

"That's what He tells us to do. He says that if we agree in prayer, He hears us and answers. He loves to hear us."

During the mid day break at the high school, the same subject was discussed by Paul and Gordon. He had only lately learned to think of this aspect of the Christian life. Now Paul mentioned that prayer for the school boys was also necessary, for, in particular, helping them with family problems, personal problems, and how to deal with their own rapidly changing bodies. Most of them were ignorant about God, his love for them, and the gospel of salvation. That Jesus' New Testament teachings could become a helpful philosophy to live by could open doors in their behaviour was a novel thought.

Paul and Gordon resolved to pray about it and ask permission from the principal for weekly meetings.

They found that the head, Mr Pringle, was indeed open to the suggestion, being very aware that teen age boys were often troubled by problems of various types. He said, "I wish you well in this ministry. At my last school a boy committed suicide, causing us grief and the question of: could we have prevented it? Choose your place and a lunch time or after school or both if you think it's warranted. You may have a three minute slot at morning assembly to announce it. Be sure to say that counselling and prayer will be confidential."

"Yes sir, thank you sir," said Paul and Gordon simultaneously. They left his office, thumbs up, and set off to pray about it.

Mari was also being rewarded for her diligence in caring for Kathy, with Sarah's help.

The headmaster of the school phoned her on Tuesday, having talked with Mrs Bennett. He was obviously sincere in his thanks for her help to Kathy and for the school to function well. "This will be kept confidential," he said, "and if we can help Mrs Spencer we'll do so."

Mari phoned Winifred with delight at the success of the venture. "I'm so pleased," said Mari. "I realise that anyone could have done this little job. But the Lord asked me to do it. I feel now that it's right for me to visit Kathy's mother. I'll be very careful what I say."

"I know you will. And even if she's embarrassed at first, she will appreciate your friendship. Yes, the Lord loves you for your obedience. We are Christ's body on earth."

Marilyn, with prayer in her heart, set out to walk to the Spencer's house, planning to be there while Kathy would be at school. She felt that this was the right day and time, guessing that they had no extra car and Mrs Spencer would be home alone.

That lady, on being told that Mari was Kathy's music teacher, received her with pleasure, and their time together was friendly and informative to Mari. She was invited to try the piano, a gift from the grandmother. "I'm so pleased that it's being used, and Kathy is thrilled to be learning. She and Sarah encourage each other. It is so good of you to teach without asking for money."

"It's just a hobby I have," said Mari lightly. "It gives me such pleasure to see the children advancing and confident. Kathy is doing well."

The next half hour was pleasant talk as two mothers together.

"Let's talk again," said Mari. "You know where I live."

She walked home while enjoying an achievement, but wondering how to fit everything into her time. However, she had pleasure in phoning Win to tell how well it had gone. "Her name is Jill and her husband is Woody, which is because his initials are WD, and he works at making wooden cupboards. Otherwise, we didn't mention him, but I think she does have needs."

"Good girl. That's a helpful start. I know you have a gift for making friends. We can pray for them. You and I might arrange a day for prayer, including them."

"Oh yes, I forgot to tell you that there is son at high school, Barry. Gordon might know him. I've invited Jill to visit me, but I really think I'd rather bring her to you."

"If you think she would like me, I would welcome her. You are very able to help her, but the more friends she has the better."

Dean was having similar thoughts too. He was attracted by the difference and the social courtesy of Paul and his family. His own father had been a charmless person, and very often in a state of intoxication.

The Chang family were always welcoming to Dean, and aware of his basic loneliness. Spending his evenings in a pub and drinking beer was not to his taste. The Chang family were intellectual and could speak on many interesting topics. Dean was intrigued by the link which they all had with the Alton family and was willing to know them better. His aunt had mentioned Marilyn Alton and had told the unhappy history of his uncle's shameful robbery from the firm.

In trying to make amends to Mari Alton for her loss, Aunt Alice suggested that Dean could help Mari with her garden, to which he agreed willingly. It was the beginning of a garden-fellowship; for which Howard also would be grateful. These evenings always ended with the invitation, "Come again, Dean. We'll see you on Sunday."

On this particular evening they all agreed to meet at St Thomas's church on the following Sunday evening, that being the venue for Professor Jeffrey Tallon's lecture on 'The Link of Cosmology with the Bible'.

Mari surprised herself by waking a little earlier than usual on a

Sunday morning, and decided to go to church, meeting Gordon and Tracy there. She enjoyed the very warm welcome, and sitting among friendly people in harmonious singing. It gave her a small thrill to see her grandson go out with the other children to Sunday school. A wise, elderly man gave a sermon which touched her heart. At the end of the service she, with Gordon and Tracy, were surrounded by the Chang family and others who welcomed them.

They were invited to stay for lunch, but Mari declined, saying that she had a husband at home to care for. "Another time, thank you,"she said, hoping to have a nap after lunch at home.

The evening loomed ahead, and Sonia and Luke Chang were busily inviting any of the lecture attendees to have supper at their home afterwards. Some ladies were offering to bring a plate of food.

"I like these people," said Mari to herself while driving home. "I think they could become real friends, even if we were broke and homeless."

The large church was full to over-flowing with people of all ages, all with an air of anticipation. There was no formality, only a welcome by the resident vicar. The distinguished scientist, Professor Jeff Tallon, spoke in a mild manner, obviously in love with his subject and wanting to share his enthusiasm without speaking down to the more or less ignorant members of his audience.

The mood was set by some clips of film taken from the observer space satellite, and with some quotes from Stephen Hawking, the famous atheistic scientist, "The Imprint of creation. The scientific discovery of the century, if not of all time." And again: "What is it that breathes fire into the equations and makes a universe for them to describe?" The many God-believing people in that audience fitted their own beliefs into those words and were happy with them.

The professor showed a photo of his own workbook, purely covered in equations. It would have been intelligible only to trained scientists, who could read it as the history of the universe from day one, when the big bang occurred fifteen billion years ago. Everyone else was reminded that God has given the Bible, a simplified version, suitable for anyone to read, as well as to understand God's greatness, His omnipotence and His love.

"We all have to confess our ignorance of *how* life began. But we Believers prefer to believe God's words, that He made us in love for the reason that He desires to have an ongoing Love relationship with us."

It was a highly appreciative audience that applauded at the finish of the professor's talk. He gave time then to answering some questions. It was agreed by all that this had been a good example of having their brains stretched.

Afterwards, the group of those invited made their way to the house owned by the Chang family. The senior members, Sonia and Luke were gracious in their welcome to a house sparsely furnished. Cups of tea were served, with a small supper. The conversation was of course, on the discourse recently heard. They sat for some time re-telling their own memories of it. Chairs were insufficient, so some of the men sat on the floor, leaning against the wall.

After a little time, a request was made to Paul to remind them of some particular parts, but he countered by saying, "I think my father should speak first. He is very well informed, and he should do so."

Luke stood slowly, a slight man, youthful looking for his sixty years. He spoke with dignity. "We who love God and have a relationship with him can believe that God has always had a plan for the universe and for the men and women He put into it, on our own special planet," he said. "I have been intensely interested," he looked towards Paul, "in the knowledge that my son has imparted to me, and what Professor Tallon has told us tonight. I feel that God is showing us favour, in these revelations. As we read in

Romans chapter one, verse twenty, 'since the creation of the world, His invisible nature and attributes have been made intelligible and discernible through His handiwork. So men have no excuse (for not believing in God).' I have been told that, in fact, the early scientists did have belief in God and in the Bible. Its truth and integrity stimulated them in the search for truth.

"In these present years some atheistic scientists would have us believe that the universe and we ourselves are the result of many chance coincidences, during millions of years. My personal experience is that I have a brain with spiritual qualities which can interact with God's Holy Spirit when I am in tune with Him in my thoughts. When we give honour and praise to Him, I believe, He can and does reward us with the tools of thought; of scientific knowledge. We've witnessed something like this in the lives of Einstein and others." Luke sat and in the brief silence his hearers broke into clapping.

Mari's glance met Winifred's, sitting across the room. She was smiling warmly, a hand lifted in satisfaction. She's glad she came, was Mari's thought.

Paul stood, and said, "After that, to add my words seem unnecessary. But yes, certainly I was taught that three hundred years ago there was only the Bible to use as a reference book, one that could be believed. There were some other more or less fanciful philosophies that attracted some people who wanted to be thought of as educated but those disappeared with time. As early as the 13th century a Franciscan monk called Roger Bacon taught that observation was the greatest way of finding truth, and the way of testing an hypothesis, together with recorded results was the method of advancing science. Truth was to be proved by the consensus of all, after honest study was valued.

"Johan Kepler was the founder of physical astronomy who believed that God the lawgiver governs the world by orderly principles. There are many famous and important scientists, including Sir Isaac Newton, who wrote firstly on the Christian faith, then mathematics. Michael Faraday studied the Bible, chemistry and brought us to electricity. James Simpson read about God putting Adam to sleep before removing his rib, then he researched chloroform. Louis Pasteur helps to keep us all well with the knowledge that we now have of bacteriology. He opposed Darwin's theory that living things generate spontaneously. They don't. The thinking of much of the world has been influenced by Darwin but not so now. We Christians believe that God created and sustains continuation of life.

"Now, perhaps I can raise a few eyebrows. Albert Einstein, a Jewish mathematician, is famous in the lifetimes of many of us. He introduced his general theory of relativity, according to which gravity is caused by the curvature of space-time. If we could travel across the universe at the speed of light, the farther we would go the less time would pass. Einstein believed the universe is so massive that it gravitationally curves space back upon itself. The change in space-time could perhaps be a cure for aging. That's my joke. Einstein has told us that the universe is much more massive than we thought. Our Milky Way is one of many galaxies. There are billions of them which exert enormous gravitational influence on galaxies millions of light-years distant. Our Milky Way is being dragged along at six hundred kilometres a second. I believe that we can trust these mathematicians who, starting from the Bible, have worked by observation, by reason and by instinctive faith."

In the hushed silenced that followed, the pastor, Adam Forester rose to his feet, saying, "What an evening, and what an amazing God we have. We can only worship and praise, knowing how privileged we are to be here, alive and with the hope that Jesus our Saviour gives us of eternal life. I propose that next Sunday morning we devote our time to speaking our praise and devotion to Him.

The music that comes to my mind is Beethoven's 'the heavens are telling'. How about spending an evening together, say Monday, for all who are interested in planning, with suggestions? I leave the choice to you people." With that he sat down, while a murmur of applause and clapping affirmed his words.

"Great idea, Pastor," said a big man sitting with his back to the wall. "I suggest we ask Mrs Marilyn Alton to come with her suggestions. She's talented and a professional musician." A murmur of approval was heard around the room.

The audience left, gladdened, for their homes.

Mari caught up to Paul, touching his arm. "Gordon tells me that you and he are praying together, with and for the students. Please could you pray for the Spencer family?" She quickly told him the story and their father's needs.

"Will do, Mari," he said. "Bless you."

On Tuesday morning, soon after nine, Mari phoned Mrs Spencer. "Would you like to have a visit with me this morning, or afternoon if you'd rather? And actually, I have another friend who has invited us both to visit her. She is a very special person, someone I love. I'd like you to meet her."

"Yes, thank you, I'd enjoy that, if you're sure she would like me to come. Morning, if that's okay with you both."

"Lovely. Shall I come and pick you up?"

"I'll walk along the beach seeing it's a fine day. Expect me soon."

If Jill was surprised to see that Mari lived in what was obviously a small beach cottage, she didn't show it. Probably the children had mentioned it already.

Win was already expecting them, and while they drove along Mari explained her friendship with her early Sunday school teacher. "She has recently helped me to build up my faith in God, when we suffered such a down turn financially that we ended up in a beach cottage. I was in despair, and when I re-established Winifred's friendship she taught me to pray to God, as I had learned, then forgotten while I was growing up. You know how we all get so busy with other things. Well, I realised that God hadn't forgotten me, and He had the right answers to my prayers, just when I needed them."

"She sounds like a lovely friend," said Jill, with some longing in her voice.

"Indeed she is. You'll meet her in a few minutes."

Win opened her door to them the moment the car pulled up. "Welcome ladies," she said, and hugged Mari. "And welcome Jill; come right in." She instinctively knew what Jill needed.

"Dear Winifred," said Mari. "You know what we want. Thank you so much for being available."

"Everyone needs love, especially Jesus' love. We might try to live without Him, then we run into insuperable difficulties. What would you like to drink now, Jill? Tea, coffee or fruit juice? And you, Mari?"

"Coffee please. And thank you for the invitation," answered Jill happily.

"Fruit juice, please. Did you make muffins so early in the morning, Win? "

"Just ten minutes to mix, then bake. I could do them in my sleep. Eat up and enjoy." As they did so, Mari noticed that Jill was relaxing and enjoying the motherly manner which to Win was natural. "Tell me about your family, Jill," said Winifred coaxingly.

She spoke a little hesitantly. "I have Kathy, she's eleven and Mari is giving her piano lessons which she loves. Barry is at High school, he's doing okay. My husband, Woody is... is..." Her face crumpled and tears ran down her cheeks. She grabbed her handkerchief, "I was so ashamed when the headmaster of Kathy's school came to see me and told me that they – the school – would pay for any extra expenses for Kathy, seeing my husband might be short of money." She sobbed a little and sniffed. "I felt I had to tell him that Woody had a job, was fairly well paid, but he gambled and couldn't stop, and borrowed to pay for our electricity bill. Then things got worse until I had almost nothing to spend on food, or for Kathy…" Jill ran out of words.

Win moved to sit beside her and wrapped her arm around Jill's shoulders. "Dear Jill, we can help you. You are having a difficult time but there are lots of things we can do to help. On short term we can get food parcels for you; longer term we can get counselling for your husband, and we shall pray for him, for healing, because gambling to that degree is a sort of disease."

Mari said, "I was telling Jill that Jesus helped me terrifically when I started to pray to Him. He works inside and outside, and gives me faith to trust Him. I know He loves me, and He loves you too, Jill. He wants me to pray and trust. Win taught me to say this out loud, so that everyone knows, without doubt."

Win was nodding, and said, "Yes, when we know we're at the bottom of the hole, and put our faith in Jesus, that's when He lifts us up. Jill dear, Jesus loves you, and He wants to help you. He has the power and strength, and you can see that you and your husband need help; well, ask Him. As He holds out His hand to you, take it by asking for His help. He wants to hear your voice. He loves you."

"I know we need help, Woody and I. But perhaps we shouldn't ask. We got ourselves into this mess."

"We all do, every one of us in this world. Tell me a little about your husband. Has he been, or tried to be, a good husband?"

"Yes, mostly. His own father wasn't a very good dad. Woody works well making things, sort of average pay. He wished he could earn more, and someone told him about backing a horse that was sure to win; so it was said. It did win, that time. Woody was so excited, he was over the moon, laughing and saying what a great system of making money. He enjoyed spending the money, of course." Jill paused, sadly. "The next time it didn't work out as well. He made only a small win. And the time after, and after that. It didn't do any good to the family. I worried about the effect on the children. Barry was watching his father. I hoped he wouldn't copy him. I began to dread the times when Woody used to hear from someone about a 'sure thing' and he'd drive to Kairua race meeting, weekends usually, but a few times he took time off work. I was scared that he'd lose his job. He almost did."

The silence lengthened.

Win squeezed Jill's shoulder and held her hand. "You poor girl. All this time you've been worried sick, and I suppose your husband wouldn't listen to you. So often they don't." She paused. "From now on we're here to help you, as I said, with the short term and longer term situation. We're asking God to help, and so we put this whole situation before Him. He has power greater than ours, and when we pray with trust we put ourselves into the place where He can work, against whatever evil things are trying to mess up your life. And we'll ask the Lord to protect your children from harm. They will learn to recognise evil and avoid it. The Lord will be your peace and your protection. Do you feel ready to talk to God now, to Jesus? They are one and the same, really, and they love you."

"Yes, Jesus, please help me, please help Woody, we want to do better and be good parents. We want to love you. Please teach us how to live."

"In Jesus' name," said Winifred.

Chapter Eleven

Woody was having a bad day. Thursday, and he had again absented himself from work to attend the race track at Kairua. The workshop was being run by the young man, his junior, who had raised his eyebrows when Woody had again taken leave. They both knew what the owner had said on that matter. However, Woody felt his pulses racing with the thought of the crowds, the voice over the loud speaker and the rush of adrenaline, while watching a certain horse. The thud of hooves, the roar of the crowd, while the sun sparkled over everyone. It would be his win, his winning prize money in his pocket, and he would go home to be congratulated.

I'm Someone! Drinks all round. What a lot of friends I have! But something had gone wrong. Here I am, driving over the green Waikato Plains, going home with my pockets empty. How can I face the owner, seeing I've taken another day off work? And my wife will probably cry because I lost all our money. You're a failure, mate.

Feeling the sourness in his stomach, he drove through the outskirts of a small town and down steep turns of the road. The big, generous river flowed through the valley before it poured its powerful flow into the lake of the power station. Millions of units of electricity to serve a million people. For lack of anything else to do, Woody drove into some free parking beside the river and stopped. It fascinated him to watch it flowing, shining dark silver, strong and

155

seeming to disregard weak people like himself. Suppose, just suppose I go into it, where would it take me? Away somewhere from my life and family. They think I'm useless anyway. The boss will sack me. No job. I've nothing to give my family. They won't want me back. I'll be gone, never found.

Two young guys were fishing under willow branches hanging over the river. "Good shade here. The fish like it. What's this rubbish floating down river? Some people are stinkers, dumping their junk; spoil a good fishing spot."

"Holy mackerel! It's a bod! Hey, d'you think it's alive? Gimme that hook; see if I can hook it's clothes. You hang onto that branch while you hang on to me, so we don't both go into the river; hang on, nearly, nearly… current's slower here… hang on; don't let me go; ah, don't let me go, nearly; half in; ah, half in; how do we get 'im up? I'll have to lie on my belly; hold my legs; damned fool weighs a ton, full of water; don't lose our line now, he's not worth it. You grab a bit so we can both pull. Stupid bugger; drag 'im away; if he slips in again we'll leave 'im. Heave! Roll 'im over, tip the water out; you know how to do mouth to mouth? Okay, take turns."

The phone rang in the police station of the small town. "Police station here. How can I help you?"

"Hey, we're two guys fishing at the river, just below the town. We've fished a chap out of the water. We tried to resuscitate him. We think he's alive, barely. He looks pretty sick. Needs some looking after."

"Okay, be there soon. Tell me how far from Cambridge. Had he a car in the car park? Right, we'll send two guys."

The welcome sound of the police siren approaching relieved the atmosphere for the fishermen. They bundled up their gear, reluctantly. "No use trying to catch fish now. They'll be a mile away. I'll go to the car park and wave them down. You wait here."

The police said, "Well done. He's alive. We might have to call an ambulance, but we're a long way from Waikato Hospital. Quicker if we take him to a doc in Cambridge, let him decide that. We'll phone ahead to let the Doc know. If that seems to be the chap's car, I'll drive it back. Just a quick statement from you guys."

On Thursday afternoon Marilyn's phone was ringing. The voice was almost hysterical. "Marilyn, I hope you don't mind me ringing you. This is Jill. Someone rang me from a town, called Cambridge. He's a doctor. My husband's there, and the doctor wants me to go and pick him up."

"Has there been an accident?"

"No, at least I don't think so. The car is there too. He needs to be driven home in the car; not well enough to drive himself. The police took him to the doctor but the car's at the police station."

"Good grief, no wonder you're worried. So you need help to be able to get there yourself."

"Yes, but I don't know who to ask. I can't pay for a taxi or anything. I don't have any money."

"Okay, let me think for a minute. I'll phone you back quickly."

"Oh dear Win, I've got a critical situation thrown at me. We need to find someone, actually two people to rescue Jill's husband from Cambridge, and drive his car back. I'm thinking of asking Gordon if he could go, as soon as school finishes. Should I go with him? I do have pupils tonight, so how do I cope?"

"It would be better to have another man. I wonder if that excellent young man Paul could be enlisted. Can he drive?"

"I think so, yes surely. It's nearly three now. I said to Jill that I'd ring her back. I'll phone her now to say that we're working on it. Bless you, Win dear and thank you for your prayers."

"I'm praying for a God-made victory in this case, and for you. You're a good servant for Jesus Christ. He'll be helping us all."

A sad and sorry-looking Woody was being driven home by Paul, while the other car was driven by Gordon. Woody was wearing his own clothes, just brought out from the dryer.

Paul said, "You've had a narrow escape, my friend. Do you want to tell me how all that happened?"

So the grim and shameful story was told.

"You've had a wake up call from God and you ought to face that. A few more minutes in that river and you'd be waking up in hell."

Woody shivered.

Paul continued, "Not a comfortable place at all, I'm told by someone who's seen it. A mean character called Satan leads men on to do stupid things like gambling. He's a liar and tells you that you can get rich quickly. He probably helped you to win the first time."

Woody said miserably, "My life's not going to be much good now. The boss said he'd sack me if I took time off again."

"Do you think," said Paul, "that he'd keep you on if you said you'd finish with gambling? If we two math teachers were going to keep our eyes on you, making sure that you keep away from all gambling?"

"Don't know. He's usually a decent man."

"You'd have to have counselling, and be reporting to the counsellor. And your wife and kids, would they want you back, as a non-gambler?"

"I hope so. I don't want to lose them."

"There is help from another source too. God is the opposite of Satan, and He is really powerful. If you give your loyalty to God, confess to Him your sinful way of life and ask Him to make you a new, clean life, He'll do that and help you with your problems."

The motor hummed peaceably along the highway. Woody mused along with it, "A new, clean life. Yes, I'd like that."

"It's a big decision for you, Woody, an important one. Jesus made the most painful sacrifice for you, for us. He saves us by His grace, and that's not cheap. If you want to say yes, we'll stop the car and you can talk to Him."

"Yes, yes I do," said Woody, loudly.

Paul drove a short distance to a widening of the road and parked.

"Jesus, God, I want to be loyal to you. I want to have a new clean life. Please take away my sins. Thank you for saving me from drowning."

"In Jesus name. Amen," said Paul.

The rest of the trip seemed to fly by. It was early evening when they arrived at Woody's home. As Paul parked, an outside light came on. Jill Spencer appeared, the faces of the children hovering behind her.

Jill's voice was sharp with worry. "Woody! What on earth have you been doing?"

Paul said, "Good evening Mrs Spencer. He's been having a swim in the river but all safe now. My name's Paul. Gordon Alton is driving your car back from the Waikato. He'll be here soon."

Jill was angry. "Woody! Have you been gambling again? What are we supposed to live on?"

"I'm sorry Jill. Never again I promise."

"He's got more to tell you, Jill. Some of it's good news. I'll leave you now. Woody, I'll say to you," he said sternly, "eat a good dinner now, with no beer. In the morning shower and shave, get to work early in decent clothes. Those look untidy. If your boss phones or arrives, tell him you are going to have counselling, with someone to vouch for your behaviour. Apologise to him. I'll say good night to you all."

"Oh wait, wait Paul, stay and have a drink and some food," said Jill.

"Well, just a few minutes until Gordon arrives. He'll drive me home."

Gordon arrived a few minutes later. Jill's thanks were effusive, while Gordon slipped something into her hand.

"The beginning of a long friendship," they agreed a little later.

Mari was nearly bursting with joy when she phoned Win the next day. "Isn't the Lord wonderful! He's given a perfect tidy up to that situation. Jill rang me this morning to tell me that Paul talked to Woody, a tough talk so he realises that he nearly went to hell yesterday. He almost drowned in the river. After which, Woody gave his life to the Lord. So now Jill's thanking God that Woody is alive, and at work, and has agreed to ask for counselling. She's praying that his boss will keep him on."

"Praise the Lord! As you say, a superb tidy up. And your Gordon and Paul did a great rescue. May the Lord bless them. We'll need to keep supporting them, with prayers and practicalities. I guess that Woody has left everything at that race track so it will take some weeks to lay up capital again."

"Yes. We can keep watch over the children to see that they'll be all right. I can ask our friend Sarah to report to me if she hears of difficulties. I hope they'll all come to church next Sunday. We'll give a special invitation."

"Excellent thought. I assume we are planning music for our celebration Sunday. And thinking about the lunch to follow. I do feel that the Lord is encouraging us this week."

"Yes, so do I. And I'm sure that Pastor's suggestion for ' the heavens are telling' is the perfect choice. I think I can persuade a real choir with a small orchestra to come to us and sing it for us. With possibly one or two other things on a similar theme."

"What a lovely thought. So we'll be having an assortment of musical pieces, is that the idea?"

"It's a sensible choice for a group of Christians, don't you think? Getting away from the formal, traditional Church as it used to be many years ago. Including children, even youngish ones as well as teenagers."

"That sounds good to me. Jesus Christ values children highly. You know, I can even imagine this becoming an annual event, as long as it involves the whole church, not just a single leader. We shall be pleasing God. We know that to praise Him is our way of keeping ourselves in the right place for living well, with Him in control."

The following Sunday morning their church was almost full, though with a set of chairs which would be occupied by the visiting choir and players. The first half hour was devoted to hymns and praise songs, with a few solos, duets and instrumental groups in well known praise songs.

The Pastor spoke next: "My friends, as you know it is my custom to be thorough, so I begin by making clear our beliefs. This God whom we praise today has always made his desires clear through his book the Bible.

"We welcome to our church people who have come from other countries, and I'm aware that some of you have heard very different teaching about what we call religion. Some of you have grown up with totally alien assumptions about how to worship God, or even who our God is. So I introduce you to the real, the only God, whom we worship as our Creator. We worship in spirit and in truth with our voices, our prayers, and our honest thoughts. Although we cannot see Him, He can read our hearts, and our minds. He is all powerful, all knowing and able to do all things. And, He loves us!

"Our salvation is *free*. By the grace of God we are offered it, thanks to Jesus Christ who took our place as the sin-bearer, a dreadful experience for Him when God laid the burden of our sin on Him. We can never know how appalling that was. But God raised Jesus to life. He now sits at the right hand of God, as our Redeemer. We owe to Him all our love, loyalty and humble service in His

Kingdom. And so we are taking this morning service in praise and worship to our God, the triune God – Father, Son (Jesus) and Holy Spirit.

"It is right that we all spend a little time in prayers of thanks to the Lord for bringing us to this day in our lives, through whatever difficulties and trials we've encountered in the time. You may speak aloud or be silent as you wish. If aloud, keep them short in order to leave time for others. We have been told recently some facts about the birth of our universe and our own planet within it. God has told us, in His word that He created our planet specifically for us. What could be more remarkable than that?"

The quiet period was allowed to continue for some fifteen minutes, after which the Pastor spoke. "We have some musical guests waiting outside to sing to us a song by Beethoven, the musical genius who believed in God. We welcome them in now. The song is titled 'The Heavens are Telling the Glory of God'." The choir and orchestra players filed in and took their seats.

The sound was indeed glorious in the old church. The acoustics did justice to the talented performers who were applauded fully by the audience. They followed by singing excerpts from the oratorio 'The Creation' by Haydn. His imaginative work told of God's creation of grass, trees, sea and living creatures. It was a feast of music, much appreciated by all. The applause was long, while the musicians made their exit.

Immediately after that, two teenagers took the microphone, a boy and a girl, reading aloud verses from the first chapter of Genesis, verses 10, 11, 12, 14 and 20. These verses say that God took the formless planet, earth, and made separation of the waters, into land and sea. He clothed the land with vegetation; plants yielding seed and trees bearing fruit with seeds after its own kind. God had said, Let the waters bring forth abundantly and swarm with living creatures and let birds fly over the earth and multiply. God had also told the earth to bring forth living creatures, animals both wild and domestic, and creeping things. After that He created human beings, "after His own image".

While the young people were reading those verses, the back door of the church was opened and two strong children entered, holding by a post at each end a long sheet of wall board. It was difficult at first for them enter successfully. But when revealed it showed a large landscape, mountains topped with snow, under a blue sky, green hills together with lush pasture land. With some help by adults the children took position in the area previously occupied by the choir. They were followed by a long line of children of all ages, the taller ones holding branches cut from trees, a few holding birds in cages, or leading small pet dogs, all very well behaved. A couple of rabbits were also led in. A small girl carried a guinea pig in a box. Danny proudly held two elegantly shaped fish which he and Grandpa had cut out of cardboard and sprinkled with silver glitter. Many children carried long-stemmed flowers. They lined up and sang the hymn "All things bright and beautiful are sent from heaven above. All creatures great and small, the Lord God made them all." Smiling adults took photos of the children enjoying the whole experience.

After the children left the church, the pastor summed up his address by saying, "We stand in awe at these marvellous revelations which so recently have given us just a hint, a glimpse of God's works. While receiving His love and redemption through Jesus we are to be His helpers, in spreading the good news to all people. Whatever we may suffer in service to Him in this world will be as nothing, so Paul tells us, compared to the rewards and the joy that God will give us when we enter His eternal kingdom." The slowly given, deep words of the pastor were allowed to sink into the minds of the congregation, who sat utterly still. "God wants us to become like Jesus. A very high aim; how can we achieve it? In Matthew 5 verse 48, Jesus says, 'You therefore must become perfect,' that is, growing into complete maturity of Godliness in mind and character, having reached the proper height of virtue and integrity, 'as your heavenly Father is perfect.'

"We are aware that this state is impossible for any of us, born into sin in a sin-damaged world. Only by humbling ourselves, taking Jesus' offer of redemption, with repentance of our former way of thought and behaviour, can we achieve it. To repent means to turn about. Our aim is to please God, with Jesus' help. We can't do it alone. Jesus teaches us the law of love; be obedient to His commands and forgive those who have hurt us, and Jesus has offered His own help, that is to be filled with His own Spirit. It is not our work but the gift of our faith in Him. He asks us to take our feet off the bottom of the pool, that being our previous knowledge, so we are water-borne, figuratively. Effortlessly, only with faith in Him, we are supported mentally and spiritually.

"The Lord may be calling you now, so I invite any or all of you to come forward to the front of the church to be blessed with our prayers, and to receive individual prayer with any of our elders, waiting here to help you with prayer if you would like it. Jesus is waiting. Those who want to have His Spirit will receive. The Holy Spirit is a gentleman who waits to be asked. Come and receive. You will be blessed."

The next half hour became fixed in the memories of those people for all the right reasons.

Mari was unable to resist the desire to share her delight and excitement about that Sunday with her friend Win. Seeing the results of prayers answered and the happy faces of people, previously in distress had her bubbling over with joy. "Did you see the Spencer family all looking so happy, and Dean being at home with friends? When Howard walked up to the front with me I was almost dancing."

Win said, "Yes, darling, I do agree it was a wonderful day. The results and rewards that God gives make one overflow with joy. Perhaps a taste of the future."

"Oh yes, Win, and the fact that Howard came and heard those excellent words of the Pastor with the call, and he responded! I'm sure that he is definitely touched by God, so this is the beginning of his new life. Danny is responsible. Howard helped Danny to make those silver fish, and he insisted that Howard come to church to see the parade of animals."

"Ah, the blessed child. In scripture it says that 'a little child will lead them'. Mari dear, it's doing me good to hear all of these details. Thank you for telling me. Now, shall we invite Jill to come and have a little prayer time this week? Suppose you and she decide on a day and time, and you let me know?"

"Yes, that will be good and necessary. I guess Paul and Gordon are cheered by Woody's week end. They'll be praying too. What an important task they are tackling."

"Yes, we share it, we work on, don't give up. Not forgetting to praise and thank the Lord. Bless you, Marilyn dear."

On the following Wednesday, Mari was still singing in her heart for the Lord's work that she could recognise as His grace. The blue skies of early summer brought the seasonal delights, in her garden and wherever she looked. She could only say, "Thank You Lord for letting me live in such a beautiful place, with the land and the sea blessing each other." I'll bring this mood to my pupils tonight, she told herself. I know how to teach them to do well, even the least gifted ones. It was so satisfying to spend a short time in her garden because Dean had done some weeding and tidying.

She was preparing a tasty dinner for her husband that night, while saying, "Thank You God," for the work He was doing in Howard's heart. I'll have the food ready and hope to have a few minutes' talk before I go out to teach.

And so she greeted him on arrival, but his first words fell into her heart heavily. "Got a new customer today," he said. "Quite a big job. He's bought an empty section in town and wants to build a TAB. He's also wanting to make a profit by doing two floors, in case the gambling game doesn't succeed; building one or two apartments on the first floor."

"Oh," was all Mari could say, while serving the dinner. Normally she would have said, "That's excellent," but a sort of hollow feeling inside was paralysing her tongue. The peace she had been experiencing earlier had departed.

"What's the matter?" he asked, sitting at the table and picking up knife and fork.

"I just don't know," she said. "I'm trying to keep my nose out of your business." They ate with no comment for a minute, until Mari said, "I'm pleased, of course. It's great that the business has been doing well. I'm very glad about everything." She paused. "Danny's doing so well too. I'm proud of him. He's tackling a vast subject, as though he were many years older, and being consistent with it. Your encouragement is just what he needs." She beamed at Howard.

"Yes," he said with enthusiasm. "Having a clever grandchild is somehow flattering, isn't it?" They both laughed. "It's a fine feeling to think that our genes are the cause!"

Mari began to prepare for her departure. "Your dessert is in the fridge. Hope you enjoy it." They had a quick hug and a kiss, as she left in her car.

Marilyn settled to practise a little before the arrival of her first pupil. The lessons were as enjoyable as usual, but in Mari's mind was a nagging doubt.

The next morning, as early as possible, she phoned her friend. "Win dear, Howard's got me worried; a big job offer involving building a TAB. He'll want to take it on, but it doesn't seem right to me to be assisting on a TAB when we've just rescued Woody from his ghastly habit. Suppose the sight of a betting shop weakens his resolve? He may think when he sees it that just a little gamble wouldn't hurt."

"Mari, you're setting a good example, and I'm proud of you. No doubt it is an attractive job for Howard. He thinks he needs it. Now, perhaps that is the way we should pray; that he will not think of it as a success for the firm, but rather that he'll turn it down because he is not fearing a shortage of funds. He knows that gambling is in itself a reckless and stupid way to act and can only cause damage to the family."

"You're right, of course, Win. I can imagine that a lot of men might be tempted to bet when the opportunity is on their doorstep. Yes, let's pray that way, and that the Lord will strengthen his conscience. Howard's had examples of that stupidity before his eyes."

"Yes, I do affirm that thinking. And while we're praying we'll ask that all of the Alton firm is showing the good profit that they hope for. We do know that they work hard for results. So we agree and the Lord hears us and blesses our prayer."

Mari worked through the rest of her day with a lightened heart, recognising many of the thoughts which flew into her mind as coming from her Lord. She found herself praying while she was working, for Howard and her family and especially for her friends who had recently come to know the Lord. As a teacher of music, she prayed for each pupil, and received ideas for them, to help them to enjoy their music and thus build up their abilities.

She had been wondering what to say to Howard when he arrived home, but he surprised her by displaying a blue and white exercise book, saying, "I went out and bought this for Danny. It's for him to keep records of his finds on the beach. I'll help him to make notes, and do the spelling, and even, if he's able, to draw what he sees. Here are the colored pens and drawing pencils. What do you think?"

With a gasp, Mari said, "Howard that's wonderful! You're a grandpa par excellence!" She kissed him. "Danny will be thrilled. We'll all be delighted at seeing this boy developing into a scientist. How lucky he is, having you to encourage him. Lots of kids will be envying him."

As Mari had few minutes to spare before she had to leave, she forgot to ask Howard about his day at work. But, as she was going out the door he said casually, "I've decided not to take on the TAB job. We've enough work as it is."

"That's good," she said, her heart bounding, and singing with joy all the evening.

Pastor Adam spoke slowly. "Today we speak about baptism, which is a symbol of a new birth, the washing away of the old life and its sins. It is an action commanded by Jesus Christ, Son of God. It is significant that it was first performed by John the Baptist who was sent by God as a forerunner, preparing the way for Jesus Christ. God's aim was to soften the peoples' hearts, by preaching to them the need for repentance. They were to learn about the new spiritual life, in communion with God. He would, Himself, lift the burden of sin, and give new knowledge into their minds. They would not be relying on the priests and their ritual of sacrificing an animal to bear the sins of people. Instead, Jesus himself became the holy sacrifice. He would carry for all time the sins of the whole world, and the Holy Spirit would be communicating personally with all men and women who asked for this amazing privilege. We are so blessed." The deep voice paused to allow the words to sink in.

"That is an enormous statement, as I'm sure you will agree," he continued. "Some of you may have heard these words many times, some not. So you can imagine the surprise, the shock, even, that the well-educated pharisees and priests felt that here they saw a young man teaching something different. They were proud men, smug in their thinking that they were God's special people, spiritually safe in their ritual of keeping the laws given by Moses, hundreds of years previously. God had sent prophets to tell them that God hated their pride; that God wanted them to humble their hearts. They killed the prophets, and they would kill Jesus, after ridiculing Him. They had not studied the Old Testament sufficiently, with faith in God."

Pastor Adam paused. "However, there were some, a few pharisees who pondered and believed Jesus' words. They had to keep a low profile in order to stay alive, such was the hatred of the majority. Joseph of Arimathea was a rich man who, after Jesus was crucified, asked Pilate for Jesus' body. As we are told, he took it, rolled it in clean linen and placed it in his own, undefiled tomb hewn in rock, with a great stone over the door. But as we now know, Jesus was raised from the dead, and exited unaided from the tomb and was seen by many. This was the beginning of our knowledge of Christianity. As He promised, He sent his own holy Spirit to be our personal Counsellor.

"I finish with one item of history which we all know about, having seen it with our own eyes and known about for many years; that the Jews became refugees, spread about many countries of the world. The Romans destroyed Jerusalem, stealing all the gold of the temple. Others followed the Romans. We know of Hitler's attempts to destroy all Jews. In 1947 the United Nations voted unanimously to restore the land of Israel to all the Jewish people, to ensure their safety. They are world news to us, and prophesies are still to be fulfilled. God hasn't finished with them yet. The time will come when we and they, Gentiles and Jews, will worship God together. We will understand each other and meet in love, as is beginning to happen already."

The sermon finished, they sang a hymn, then greeted one another with love and began to disperse. Mari and Howard drove home quietly in thought.

"What did you think of that?" Mari asked her husband.

"Interesting," he said. "Quite a lot to think about. The history part is enlightening. I'm learning."

On the following Tuesday, the firm's accountant entered Howard's office with the bank's balance sheet in his hand. Howard frowned a little.

"What now?" he asked, expecting the worst.

But Gren was smiling, with some amazement. "See here, we've got a bonus, an entry of $15,000! I couldn't believe it, sure that someone's made a blooper. There's no name, so I phoned the bank in question and yes, they told me, it's true! It's from the account of a customer who wants to be nameless."

Howard's eyes opened wide in disbelief. "A gift? Such things don't happen!"

"It is indeed correct," said the accountant. "We checked everything."

"Well, pigs might fly. I'll ask my wife if she has any rich friends. Some friends!"

"Well, it's improved our situation nicely. So long as it doesn't disappear tomorrow." He left the room happily.

On the following Sunday morning, an air of expectation filled the church.

Pastor Adam spoke. "We are blessed that ten people are here today, desiring that they will be baptised. As I told you last Sunday, we are obeying God's command in that, whoever becomes a believer in Jesus Christ will follow our Lord in baptism. This is a symbolic action which shows openly that this is the beginning of a new spiritual life, the old life being washed away. I remind you that, as a ritual it does not change our spiritual condition, only God knows that. But He knows our hearts, and He will bless our obedience."

The stage was prepared, by removal of the baptism cover, showing waist-high warmed water. Pastor Adam and an elder appeared, wearing shorts, with the ten candidates, suitably clothed, who were invited, one by one, to enter the water. They were held safely, plunged quickly in, and were released, dripping water. Most of them were smiling. Each time the words were intoned by an elder: "We baptise you (named) in the name of God the Father, the Son, and the Holy Ghost." Praise songs to God were being sung throughout. The candidates for baptism were waiting in a queue.

When it was the turn of Woody to descend into the water, the Pastor raised his hand to signal a pause. Smiling, he said, "Our next friend has a special reason to thank God, which he wants to tell you himself."

Woody stepped into the water, his face beaming, and said, "I wouldn't be here today but for the fact that God saved my life a week or two back. I had made such a mess of my life, gambled my money and I was on the point of losing my wife and my job. I parked beside the Waikato river and jumped into it to be drowned but two guys fished me out and saved my miserable life. Paul Chang and Gordon Alton rescued me and told me that God had a much better alternative for me, so here I am. I've confessed to God and my wife. She's been an angel, forgiving me, and she's here today." He looked back to her standing there, and they both were radiant.

The pastor said, "Yes indeed, Jesus is the living water."

After the splash, Woody climbed the steps and still trailing water, hugged Jill and kissed her. The congregation cheered and clapped a little.

A male voice shouted, "Praise the Lord!"

Mari, the last to be baptised, came out with saturated fair hair and a big smile on her face. They dried and returned quickly to their seats, Mari and Howard together holding hands. All the children had been in church, watching these proceedings. Now, they were escorted to their classrooms by their teachers.

Pastor Adam, now dry also, rose to speak. "This is a joyous occasion and one to be taken seriously in the eyes of God and the world. New beginnings require thought. We are challenged to become like Jesus Christ, and that means changing our thinking. I believe that this is to be an ongoing, a learning process for every person, old and young, including myself. God wants us to grow spiritually. We are challenged to do so, 'don't remain as babes in the word.'

"One important thing comes to mind: repentance. As for these newly baptised people today, let us remember that we all may need to do some repenting at various times in our lives. It is linked with the process of God working in us, the process of sanctification. David was probably thinking of this when he wrote, Search and know me, oh God, see if there be any evil way in me. Psalm 139:23,24."

The pastor paused, then allowed a big smile to illuminate his face. "Those are the hard words," he said. "Now we file those away into the appropriate places in our brains, and celebrate with the Lord's supper. Jesus told His followers to do this, in remembrance of Him, on His last night on this earth."

Adam picked up his Bible and read aloud from Matthew 26, verse 26. "Now as they were eating, Jesus took bread; when He had broken it He gave it to the disciples, saying, Take, eat, this is My body broken for you. And He took a cup of wine, and gave it to them, saying, Drink of it, all of you. For this is My blood of the new covenant, which is being poured for many, for the forgiveness of sins."

The partaking of the bread and wine, after thanks, was done with all reverence. Lastly, they all sang a hymn in praise of Jesus.

The social hour and lunch that followed were blessed with an atmosphere of love and praise after the display of obedience and church unity. It was a delightful family celebration.

Pastor Adam made a point of speaking to Mari and Howard, acknowledging their gifts to the community and Marilyn's contributions on the previous Sunday. She, remembering her past experiences of entertaining 'friends' whose motives were far different, recognised a vast contrast and a trust in these, their new friends.

Howard also could sense a comfortable relationship with them. Yes, he thought, no one is perfect but I believe these people are trying to please God, and I like them.

Many of these new acquaintances knew already about Marilyn's gifts being shared freely, and knew that the firm 'Alton Electrics' was of high quality.

The children were having a wonderful time, chasing about the big room but now and then being reprimanded by their parents for their boisterous behaviour. With all the noise, movement and socialising, Tracy and Marilyn were not aware for a little time that Danny was absent. Questioning the Chang family revealed that Chen also was missing. Gordon and Paul immediately departed to hunt for them.

After walking a little distance, Gordon paused, and said, "I wonder if… there's a place near here… my brother and I were naughty one day and discovered a tip – the sort of place you don't want your kids to get into. Fascinating to boys, of course. Shall we try it?"

With unspoken agreement they set off with rapid strides, both thinking darkly of what they would say to the brats. Sure enough, when they reached it they could see one black-haired head and one blond at the bottom of a very steep bank, on a messy and unhealthy looking rubbish dump.

Both men bellowed, and to enforce their words they descended the difficult track.

Two pairs of innocent eyes met theirs. "We were just…" started one lad, but their hands were gripped by two angry men, who hustled them up the bank. "…collecting wood to make a house," panted the other boy.

"You just wait till your mothers see you, filthy little brats! And our trousers and shoes all have to be cleaned before we can go to work tomorrow," snarled Gordon.

There was no doubt that two boys were penitent when faced by irate mothers and grandmothers, and dragged into the washroom. Several little girls were snickering at the sight.

Marilyn was sitting quietly in a chair, having been denied entrance to the kitchen where the ladies were still finishing the lunch dishes. She felt her heart was overflowing with thanksgiving as she saw Howard, Gordon and Tracy talking to a couple of their new friends. Danny was bouncing about still, uncaring about his dirty appearance. The Chang family had made her feel completely at home, as had Jake and his family. Interestingly, that family had naturally linked with the Spencer family. Two tradesmen together; she smiled at the match.

Amazingly, even Rodney had come, probably coerced by his present girl friend, a pretty, thoughtful student of architecture. Not the flirty type to which he was usually attracted. Consuela seemed genuinely interested in a church ceremony, as she said, and was charming to Mari, who was pleased and equally charming. Sylvia had come with Gordon and was chatting animatedly with someone her own age. Dean had brought his Aunt Alice, who appeared to be happily entertained by some of the church ladies.

Winifred was comfortably seated in the only soft chair, with sleeping Melissa in her lap. She and Mari exchanged smiling glances, probably thinking similar thoughts. This is a God-made set of new beginnings.

Chapter Twelve

"Winter solstice, the shortest day," said Mari happily. "Tomorrow will be longer and the next and the next. Someone may think me batty, but I'm allowed to talk to myself in my own garden. Next summer is on the way."

She had pulled on a jacket for the breeze was chilly although the sun shone. Wearing old shoes she walked around her garden, or what remained of it. Now, joy of joys, the foundation for their new house was in place, poured in rock-like concrete by the master builder, Jake, of the horny hands. A few steps led up to what would be the entrance. The last pour had been done on Saturday, previously, and Mari had seen the result when she arrived home from a day of teaching.

Her excitement getting the better of her, she ran around the men, hugging and kissing each grimy face, while they grinned, thumbs up, in triumph. Today she felt she was nearly bursting with happiness, singing and dancing while thanking God. Breathless, she leaned against the wall of the old building and closed her eyes.

In her mind she saw plainly the house as Ben planned and drew it; the simple straight lines of a modern Mediterranean house, deceptively simple, for the immaculate internal planning would give all comfort and up to date inventive practicalities using solar heating and storage of electricity. In white cladding it would be striking against a background of lush green New Zealand trees.

But it won't be a show home, it'll be our pleasant, full of love home. Thank you, Lord, you had this planned for us, long ago. Thank you for bringing us to this moment in our lives.

The ringing phone broke Mari's reverie, and she dropped her muddy shoes at the door as she ran in.

Winifred's voice spoke. "Mari dear, how are you?"

"I'm full of happiness for what the Lord is doing for us; this special house is real! The foundations are laid; last Saturday was the completion. I've been outside, muddy feet and all, dancing and singing to the Lord. Jake has been working Saturdays on it, while finishing another job, with his apprentice. In a few weeks he'll be our full time builder. On the Saturdays he's been helped by Howard, Gordon, Rodney and Woody. Even the younger boys have hung about to help. I'm so pleased to see Barry Spencer and Jake's Peter being good friends. Oh yes, Dean helped one day and his auntie sent scones for morning tea. Consuela, the architectural student is often here being interested. I'm delighted to see her and Rodney together." Marilyn stopped to take a breath.

"Wow! That is something major to report!" said Winifred. "No wonder you are dancing and singing. God must be pleased with that response by you. That's the sort of thing He encourages, if you read the Old Testament. King David was that type. I love it. I could guess you've had no trouble raising a mortgage?"

"None at all. The bank says we're healthy, the firm's doing okay, and I earn my few cents. I'm so looking forward to having a moving-in party, maybe in four to five months; with my piano in our new house. We might have people visiting, sent by other architects, because this house will be unique in our country. That's all right. It won't bother me. We owe it to Ben, to advertise his work. I'm proud of it, for Ben's sake, and for the Lord. People know what happened last year, our fall into poverty: now I tell every one I know how God has done this for us."

"That's absolutely true, Mari, it's a testimony that speaks volumes. I've watched you being obedient all along, giving praise and thanks for everything. You're generous with your time, you've helped the Cobbold boy and made a friend of his aunt. And the others: you've been a busy woman and done so many things in Jesus' name. You're a worthy disciple of Jesus. As He told us, each Spirit-filled Christian is a temple of God, and collectively we are like a building, a structure, to which the needy can go for help."

"The needy; that means whatever the need, doesn't it?" said Mari reflectively. "What God has done for me. I was at the bottom of an awful hole; I could never get out on my own."

"Yes, when God works in our lives He can give us the most amazing results. If, when at the bottom of a hole, we hand the control completely to Him, He will grasp us and lift us up, victorious. If we ask Him He will come to us. That's when hope is born."

"I do thank you heaps, dear Win, for helping me as you have. And for telling me so nicely that I've accomplished something. You do me good."

"Thank you for giving me the opportunity. It's my pleasure."

"Win, I love you, and please come to our house warming party."

"I wouldn't miss it. By that time you'll have made so many more friends, there'll be standing room only."

"Oh, lovely, real friends. So long as they bring their own chairs, I'll enjoy it."

The end.

Appendix

Bible Verses Referred to in this Book

Chapter 2

We are made worthy by the redemption of our sins by Jesus' blood. Ephesians 1:7.

Satan, in his pride, tempted Eve in the garden of Eden, to disobey God. Genesis 3:5,6.

Adam and Eve became rebels. Genesis 3.

Satan (the invisible spirit) wages war against God. 11 Corinthians 10:4.

Grace to help in every need, in Jesus' Name. Hebrews 4:16.

Jesus is always living to make intercession (for us) to God. Hebrews 7:25

Chapter 3

Pray (for God's help) and He works with us. Romans 15:5.

Spirit-filled. Acts 2:4.

Ever-present help. Acts 2.

Richer, fuller life (quiet joy deep down). Galatians 5:22.

Sanctification (perfection of our spirit, by God). 1 Peter 1:2.

God reads our hearts. Matthew 5:8.

God wants us to pursue Him. 1 Timothy 6:11.

Chapter 5

He is my shelter. Psalm 61:4.

I will never leave nor forsake you. John 14:18.

Our future, God's control. Psalm 145:19.

Put family into God's hands for protection. Ezra 8:22.

Pray and praise God without ceasing. Psalm 138:1&2.

Any person who knows what is right to do but does not do it, to him it is sin. James 4:17.

The Lord's supper, holy communion. Matthew 26:26-28.

I will watch over them, to build, says the Lord. Jeremiah 31:28.

Jesus wants us to grow into complete maturity of godliness in mind and character. Matthew 5:48.

Then you will seek Me and find Me when you search for Me with all your heart. (God's words.) Jeremiah 29:13.

Lessons from the Book of James

The letter of James may be the earliest of the New Testament letters. He is probably the brother of Jesus. He is concerned with the practical ethical life, a Christian life in which our behaviour proves our faith in God, in equal proportions; that we may be perfectly and fully developed, v4 in chapter 1. I believe that this is a most important document for the teaching of everyone, Christian as well as non-Christian. The carrying out of this advice would prevent an enormous amount of mental and emotional pain which blights an incalculable number of people. Counsellors report this to be so. I speak of the results of an undisciplined tongue. James calls it a fire, a spark of which can set a forest alight. It can destroy a church. Even within so-called Christian families this can continue unchecked. A middle-aged woman is still afraid of an older brother with a certain tone in his voice. A respected church elder may have a wife who walks on tiptoe behind him, fearing his anger.

Children who are told critically destructive, personal remarks can grow up in a state of hopeless despondency, in fact a curse, which needs to be broken by Jesus.

But (James tells us) the wisdom from above is first of all pure, then it is peace-loving, courteous and gentle, full of compassion and good fruits, impartial and unfeigned. The harvest of righteousness is the fruit of the seed, sown in peace by those who work for and make peace; towards accord, agreement and harmony between individuals, in a peaceful mind free from fears and moral conflicts (v17, v18).

A Note from the Author

When I was just six years old I realised that I was *down*, very low, though not understanding the reasons for it.

In the school holidays, my parents and I went to visit my aunt. She made the observation, "That child's always crying."

My mother glanced at me without comment. In the next hour or two, as I thought about it, I realised the reason for the tears was that I knew my father and my mother both rejected me; in fact they were physically neglecting me, which was obvious to schoolteachers and others. I knew I was alone. They wouldn't change.

That was eighty years ago.

I had heard of an amazing God whom my grandmother had worshipped. She was a lady much admired and respected for her successful life, after leaving Ireland in dire poverty. Sadly, she died when I was three and a half, but I had heard the stories about her. I decided that I would worship her God, and He began to counsel me.

In spite of grief and rocky experiences along the way, I am aware of God's support in my long life, giving me the victory in many testing experiences. He is my Security, my Guide and my loving Comforter. He always hears and answers my prayer.

This book is dedicated to
Pastor Grant Hynds and Winifred Hollister-Jones

www.ingramcontent.com/pod-product-compliance
Lightning Source LLC
Chambersburg PA
CBHW070320120726
47909CB00008B/2525